AND OTHER FILTHY TALES OF LOVE

LAURELIN PAIGE

Hot Alphas. Smart Women. Sexy Stories.

Be sure to **sign up for my newsletter** where you'll receive **a FREE book every month** from bestselling authors, only available to my subscribers, as well as up-to-date information on my latest releases.

PRO TIP: Add laurelin@laurelinpaige.com to your contacts before signing up to be sure the list comes right to your inbox.

DID YOU KNOW...

This book is available in both paperback and audiobook editions at all major online retailers! Links are on my website. If you'd like to order a signed paperback, my online store is open several times a year here.

DIRTY FILTHY VALENTINE

ONE

"WHAT DID DONOVAN GET YOU? I bet it was super romantic. Tell me all the details so I can gush in jealousy."

I shifted the receiver from one ear to the other, uncomfortable with Audrey's conversation starter. What had I expected though? It was February 14th and this was my little sister. She worshipped at the altar of St. Valentine all year long. The official holiday was the one day she could expect everyone else to see the world through love-colored glasses along with her.

And since this was the first time I'd actually had a "boyfriend" on the date—if that's what Donovan was to me—of course she'd be eager to hear all about it. If I hadn't wanted to deal with her whimsy, I shouldn't have accepted the call when Ellen patched it through.

"Oh, you know him," I said, trying to sidestep the quick-sand that I was already sinking in. "He's not really a hearts and flowers kind of guy."

"That's right. His gift was probably something super erotic. Is he taking you away for a sex weekend? Did he buy a new contraption for your secret sex dungeon?"

"Audrey!" I tried to glance out the door, worried about who might overhear me. Since Donovan was technically my boss—or rather, the owner of Reach, Inc., the marketing firm where we worked—it was even more crucial to keep the details of our relationship on the down-low around others in the office. But since I didn't have a vantage of the hall from my desk, the neck straining was unproductive.

I lowered my voice, and angled my chair toward the corner of my office, as if that might protect me from eaves-droppers. "We don't have a secret sex dungeon. Could you please stop assuming we're some BDSM couple from one of those trashy romance books you read?"

Her sigh was filled with swoon. "You mean one of those incredible, amazing, romance books I read." With a sharper tone, she added, "You know, Sabrina, for a feminist, you aren't very supportive of women's choices when they aren't your own."

Immediately I felt guilty. Truth was that I had no prob-lems with her romantic notions. I even indulged in a sexy novel on occasion. Criticizing her reading material was a knee-jerk reaction to the stress of the conversation. "You're right. I didn't mean that. I just don't know where you get your ideas about my relationship with Donovan. We don't have a dungeon. We don't have a playroom. We don't even have a set of handcuffs."

"Fine. I'm not going to try to pretend I understand what it is you're into, but I know it's kinky, so you stop trying to pretend otherwise and tell me what he got you. Or, if it's too personal, can you at least hint?"

It was my turn to sigh, but it was less swoon and more resignation. Sex with Donovan was definitely kinky, but I was hard pressed to try to define what it was we were into. What it was *I* was into. I was only just becoming comfortable with my preferences myself, thanks to the man who'd taken my virginity more than ten years ago and had only just recently come back into my life. Not only did he know what I needed—dirty, filthy, rough play with dubious consent—but he'd also encouraged me to accept that I wasn't weird because of it. I was a normal, healthy, sexually vibrant woman who loved a man who understood me better than I understood myself.

I wasn't about to tell my sister any of that.

But, even if I was okay with talking to her about my sexual proclivities, that wasn't the underlying frustration with this tête-à-tête.

Again, I glanced back toward the door. Then I glanced at the clock on my computer. It was a quarter to five, which meant there would be a lot of activity in the halls with the office closing up soon.

"Hang on a sec," I said to Audrey. I set the receiver on the desk and hurried over to the entrance of my office. I glanced around to see if anyone seemed to need me, exchanged a smile with Ellen, then shut the door before darting back to my desk.

Now feeling sure that what I said would remain private, I launched into my complaint. "He didn't get me anything, Audrey."

There was a silence that I sensed was stunned. "What do you mean he didn't get you anything?"

"I mean *he didn't get me anything*. Nothing romantic. Nothing sexy. No trips for the weekend. No flowers. No chocolate. Not even a card. Nada. Zip. Nothing." I hated how disappointed I sounded over it—how disappointed I *felt* over it. Audrey was the one who believed that those kinds of sentiments were meaningful. Not me.

Yet, as deliveries had come in throughout the day for my coworkers, as Ellen had bragged about the new earrings her girlfriend had given her, as I'd had a sneezing fit from all the flowers perched on desks when I walked down the hall, I'd deflated. Was I being ridiculous or were these gestures something I genuinely needed from a partner? Donovan and I were compatible on almost every level, but was it possible we didn't speak the same love language?

"I don't believe it." Audrey-the-ever-optimist was unwilling to face reality. "That guy is too into you not to do anything for you. Do you think he forgot what day it was?"

Donovan wasn't the type to forget anything. He was the most observant person I'd ever met, and his attention to detail was exceptional. Those were cold hard facts.

But in case Audrey thought my perception of his character traits was shaded by my feelings for the man, I had other proof to offer. "If he forgot before he woke up today, he knew shortly after. I gave him my Valentine's card first thing."

As well as a blowjob. He'd been much more appreciative of the latter. To the card, which had contained a short but very personalized note about my feelings for him, he'd simply said, *"That's a cute declaration of something I already know."*

"Then he's going to do something for you tonight!" My sister's idealistic vision had no end. "The day isn't over yet. Just wait."

"I don't know about that. He was blatantly unimpressed with my—"

Without warning, my office door opened, and the man in question stepped in, shutting the door again behind him.

I could feel my cheeks heat, even though there was no way anything he could have heard me say was embarrassing. It was just as likely that it was my irritation at his intrusion that was behind the rush of blood to my face.

"Uh, hey, sis, I have to go. Talk to you soon, okay?" I didn't wait for her to respond, though I did hear a final insistence that Donovan surely had something up his sleeve as I lowered the receiver toward the cradle.

Not very likely, as far as I was concerned, but a girl could certainly hope.

"The door was shut for a reason," I said to my lover, a mock scowl on my face as I stood to come around my desk. "What if I'd been with a client?"

He shrugged dismissively. "Ellen told me you were on the phone with your sister, so I already knew it wasn't business related."

"Just because it wasn't business doesn't mean it wasn't private."

He smirked. "You and I both know you relinquished your privacy the minute you stepped into the threshold of my room at The Keep."

That had been more than ten years ago, and I *hadn't* known it for the greater part of the decade. But I did know it now, and his point was clear. Why would I ever think that a shut door would be an obstacle for Donovan Kincaid?

I crossed my arms over my chest and pretended to pout. "We could have been planning something special. You would have ruined the surprise."

"Good thing you weren't planning anything then. Especially since I hate surprises, unless I'm the one doing the surprising."

The pessimism I'd expressed with Audrey started to melt away. Had she been right? Was he about to spring me with a Valentine's Day surprise? It was still a little before five. Donovan wasn't the type to leave his desk early without a good reason.

My pulse kicked up in anticipation as his hazel eyes grew dark and his rugged features stern. "Get over here so I can figure out whether or not you're wearing panties under that skirt. It's been driving me crazy all day."

With no reluctance, I stepped into him, relishing the feel of his arms as they came around me, and his lips met mine with a possessive kiss.

After several delicious strokes of his tongue and enough groping of my ass to get me hot and bothered, he broke away. "A thong? I can't decide if I'm disappointed or excited about the extra barrier between me and your cunt."

"Barriers have never been a deterrent for you."

"No, they haven't."

Liquid heat pooled between my legs. "That gleam is a wicked gleam, Mr. Kincaid. Are you suggesting I break my rule about no fooling around at the office?" It was a rule he frequently ignored, and, considering I had no resistance where Donovan was concerned, one I'd broken a few times myself.

He kissed me again, much shorter this time and without as much tongue. "I wish I could, Ms. Lind. Unfortunately, I came to tell you I'm going to be home late tonight. The new client Nate brought in wants to meet with both of us at The Grand Havana Room before he signs the contract."

"*Tonight?*"

"Short notice, I'm sorry. You know how Trent Advertising is swarming over this one. Gotta get it signed before we can call it a victory."

My entire body went rigid. I pushed out of his arms so he wouldn't notice. "But it's Valentine's Day."

He shrugged a single shoulder. "I take it these boys don't celebrate."

Obviously a lot of boys didn't celebrate.

"They must have very understanding wives and girlfriends," I said coolly. "Or no women in their lives at all."

"I'm pretty sure Cooper is gay." Whoops. There I was assuming things based on my heterosexual lens. "And whether or not his boyfriend understands has very little bearing on how business actually works. We don't get to take days off for our birthdays either. It's called being grown-up."

My scowl this time was very real. "Thank you for the mansplaining." I sat on the edge of my desk, my arms once again crossed over my chest. "So you're going to be drinking and smoking cigars with the boys, and I should fend for myself for dinner, that's what you're telling me? In that case, I think I'll stay here and get some work done while the building is quiet."

I did have work to do—at a company as successful as

Reach and since I'd recently been promoted to the Director of Marketing, I *always* had work to do. However, I'd made the comment as a dig to Donovan who didn't like it when I stayed late alone.

And since it was a holiday that all the other execs in the office were likely to celebrate, I would most definitely be alone if I stayed tonight.

"Make sure you order something for dinner," he said, surprising me with his choice to not push back. "I'll tell the security guards you're up here. And you'll set the alarm when everyone else is gone."

My response was terse. "Yes. I'll set the alarm."

He studied me for a handful of seconds, while I tried not to study him. He was stunningly attractive on an average day, even more so wearing his fitted cashmere Kiton suit, the brown of the jacket bringing out the dark flecks in his eyes. Paired with the taupe-gray trousers and his leather Berluti shoes, it was impossible not to want to jump him. Or, more specifically, for *him* to jump *me*.

That wasn't happening, though. At least not tonight.

"Hey," he said, stepping forward so he could rest his palm at my neck. "I know I got you riled up with the heavy petting when I first came in, and I definitely owe you payback for this morning. I don't like it either when I have to put work before you. I'll make it worth the wait. Okay?"

It was a sweet gesture, authentically Donovan. It made me feel guilty for being disappointed. This was who he was— responsible and practical. It wasn't his fault that I thought today he might be different. It was a stupid, trivial commercial holiday created by marketers like me. I knew better than to put any meaning behind it. I definitely knew better than to expect that *he* would put any meaning behind it.

But knowing all that and feeling guilty about it didn't change the fact that I was still disappointed. Donovan used words of love so sparingly, I'd kind of been looking forward to today. Wondering how he'd express his feelings, what kind of gift he'd give. What his version of a romantic card would entail.

I wasn't just disappointed, I was crushed.

Our first Valentine's Day as a couple, and we'd be spending it apart. While the waitresses and gay men at the gentlemen's club drooled over Donovan in his bespoke suit, I'd be putting together Conversion Metrics Reports.

Lucky, lucky me.

TWO

ALMOST THREE HOURS LATER, I shoved my chair away from my desk and blinked a few times. I'd been staring at my screen too long, and now my eyes were dry. Donovan had told me to stop for dinner, but I hadn't, half because I'd been too wrapped up in work, but also half out of spite.

As my stomach growled loudly, I realized I was the only one suffering from that decision.

Resigned to the fact that I had a human body with human needs, I stood up and stretched. Then I padded my way down the hallway toward the kitchen in search of some forgotten leftovers in the fridge. If I couldn't find anything edible, I could always resort to one of the many options for takeout that Ellen had tucked away in one of her drawers.

Reach, Inc. occupied two floors of the Town Center. The executive offices were on the sixtieth floor, and with floor-to-ceiling windows on all sides, there wasn't a direction you could turn without bumping into a stunning view. Even at night, there was so much to see and wonder over in New York City. *Especially* at night.

But at this hour in the heart of the office away from the windows and the light pollution, the darkness was thicker. The space was my home-away-from-home, and generally I felt very comfortable in it, but this was my first time alone like this, and it was thus unexpectedly creepy. The hallway was only dimly lit from floor lights that ran along both sides, and my mind played tricks, convincing me that every shadow was a hidden predator, making me jump every time the ceiling whooshed with the sound of the heat turning on.

With a shiver, I pushed the swinging door into the kitchen and flipped the light off and on several times before remembering that most of the office's lighting was shut off when the alarm was set. I groaned, wishing I'd brought my cell phone with me from my office. I debated for several seconds about returning to get it before deciding I was too lazy. Instead, I pushed the swinging door open, using the dim light it let in to run to the refrigerator before the door shut again.

Unfortunately, a brief scan of the contents of the fridge said it had been cleaned out recently. I found nothing edible beyond a jar of maraschino cherries, sardines, and several cans of tomato juice. I'd have to look through Ellen's menus for something. Or, at this point, I might as well go home and eat something there, though with transportation the way it was in the city, that would mean almost another hour with a grumbling stomach.

With another groan, I slammed the fridge, forgetting that I'd be left in the dark when the light shut off with it closed.

Now I had to get back to the kitchen door in the pitch-black dark.

This night just gets better and better.

I stumbled my way toward the door, holding onto the counter until I got to the wall, then used that to get back to where I'd come in. It was a relief to push the door back into the dimly lit hallway, despite coming up empty-handed on my mission.

As immediately as the relief came, it vanished when a rustle came from somewhere down the hallway in the direction of the stairwell.

I froze, listening. Nothing.

Then I heard it again.

The hair stood up on the back of my neck. I was alone and unarmed. Should I go back into the kitchen and try to find a knife? It would take too long in the dark.

Besides, the alarm was set and there was no way anyone could be in the office. I was imagining things, turning innocent noises into nonexistent threats.

But as I started down the hallway, I heard the sound again.

I stopped, straining my ears. It could be the cleaning crew, though they weren't due to arrive for another couple of hours. Very few employees had the alarm code, and even fewer would use it at this time of night. Was it possible that someone hacked their way in?

No. Very unlikely. They'd have to hack the whole building's security system to get past the guards, and that was even less likely.

Oh, that's who it probably was—the security guard. Donovan had said he'd tell them to keep an eye on me.

Reassured by my reasoning, I set out down the hall again. "Hello?" I called out, not wanting to startle the guard when I wasn't where expected. "Anybody there?"

When nobody answered, goosebumps erupted down my arms.

I refused to be scared of nothing, though, so instead of cowering I marched toward the stairs to look around.

No one was there.

The door to the stairway was still closed. I reached for the handle but didn't turn it. If it was the guard, he'd have a key to open the door and a passcode for the alarm. If it wasn't the guard and the alarm was still on, opening it would set it off. Which might be a good thing if whoever might be on the other side was a danger.

But most likely there was no one on the other side, and then the alarm would be a hassle.

I put my ear to the door and listened.

Nothing. It was a thick concrete door, though. What did I expect to hear?

This whole thing was silly, anyway. The alarm was on, the sound had stopped, and I was getting myself worked up over nothing.

Convinced I had an overactive imagination, I walked toward the beckoning light of my office.

I had almost made it to Ellen's desk before the rustle returned as someone pounced and grabbed me from behind. A gloved hand covered my mouth before I could even think of letting out a scream.

THREE

"THIS WILL BE EASIER on you if you don't struggle."

The voice was a low, harsh whisper in my ear, unrecognizable without its tone. I could feel fabric where the man's cheek met mine. He was probably wearing a ski mask.

I'd been in this position before. Not once, but twice. Been caught alone with a man who wanted to defile me without my consent. The terror was like pain—it was hard to remember how bad it was unless I was in it, scared and shaking, my heart galloping against my chest.

When I wasn't actually in the clenches of a bad man, that kind of fear aroused me. It confused me to want the fantasy of it like I did, when I knew how horrific the reality was.

The usual panic settled on me now, causing my palms to sweat and my pulse to skyrocket, but, while the situation was horrifying, I somehow felt...safe?

With nothing to prove my gut instinct, the wisest thing to

do was fight, and so I did, struggling against the tight, familiar grip. I jerked to the right, then quickly swerved left and down. And that's when I saw his shoes—brown leather Berlutis.

Donovan.

Dismay became excitement. Fear became elation. Adrenaline still coursed through my veins, but now it was powered by exhilaration. Donovan was playing a game, a game I liked very much. Audrey was right—he hadn't neglected Valentine's Day.

And he knew exactly the kind of gift I'd like best.

Strangely, once I knew the man was Donovan, my fight began in earnest. I knew he wouldn't hurt me for struggling the way a stranger might. He'd fight back, but he wouldn't really hurt me. He'd just get more turned on.

Abruptly, I lodged my right elbow back into his sternum. His hand dropped from my mouth as he bent over, letting out a gasp that sounded more full of irritation than pain. With one side of my body free, I veered left, using the momentum to try to escape the grasp of his other hand.

It worked. I was free, and I ran toward my office. I could shut him out and lock the door if I made it inside without him catching me.

Of course, I wanted to be caught. But I didn't have to *let* him. He'd get me in the end, no matter what.

In fact, I didn't make it more than three steps before he launched forward and grabbed at my dress. I didn't care if it tore, and I pulled against his grip, but the fabric was too strong, and he was easily able to hold on. As soon as I realized it, I spun in toward him, hoping to catch him off guard with my sudden change of movement as I lifted my hand to strike him across the face.

He was too quick. He caught my hand in the air. His other hand let go of my dress and grabbed my other wrist before I could hit him from that angle. I lifted my knee instead, aiming nowhere in particular, using whatever means I had to defend myself. He raised his own knee across his pelvis, just in time to block mine, then he pushed it forward and into me, tackling me to the ground underneath him.

"Too easy," Donovan said, this time with his full voice, and if I hadn't known it was him before this, I certainly did now.

The victory in his tone fueled another burst of energy. With a hard yank, I managed to get one hand free. I used it to push the base of my palm hard against his jaw. Automatically, he lifted up, and it was just enough for me to be able to turn and get out from underneath him.

But then I was on my side. From there, he wrenched my captured hand behind my back with a growl, and when he caught the other again, he yanked it to my back as well. I could hear his rapid breaths as he held me there, pinned using one hand and his knee.

After several seconds of nothing, I glanced over my shoulder to see he was looking around the room. I discovered what he was looking for a moment later when he used his free hand to tug sharply at the cord that led from the wall to the phone on Ellen's desk. The wall end came out easily. When he pulled the other end, the entire phone came, skidding across the desk before it banged to the ground where he could easily drag it close enough to maneuver the cord out from its socket.

Once he had the cord free, he wrapped it several times around my wrists until they were bound, then he flipped me over onto my back. Pinning me down with his hips, he held himself above me, his arms extended. "Get it out of your system?"

I could tell he was smirking, even with a mask over his face. "Fuck you."

"I'm planning to fuck *you*, actually."

God, yes.

"No, please. Please. Please, don't." I'd never tried begging before when we'd played this.

His eyes darkened and his breaths shallowed. His pelvis was pressed flush to mine so I could feel every inch of the solid column of flesh hidden under his clothes. It seemed to grow thicker with my pleading. My pussy ached in response. I was wet with arousal, my clit buzzing as erotic organ called out to erotic organ, a primal mating song.

Why did I get off on this so much? The fantasy, the fight, the force, the fuck. It was my favorite way to make love, and as crazy as it seemed to say that, I knew that was exactly what this was for him too—making love. Using our physical bodies to express an emotion we both felt in abundance for the other. While I could never know the whys of what made my libido light up, I did know for certain that he and I were meant to be.

"While your begging is quite lovely, I'm not going to change my plans. I can smell your cunt from here, and I can already tell it's too sweet to pass up." He pushed himself up to a kneeling position and took off his gloves before undoing his belt. He'd changed to jeans, I noticed now, paired with the rust button-down mock turtleneck sweater I'd given him for Christmas. He was as enticing in casual as he was dressed up.

Involuntarily, my tongue flicked out along my bottom lip.

You're supposed to not want this, I reminded myself.

"I'll scream," I said when he lifted his ass up to pull his jeans and underwear down. Fuck, he was beautiful like that —dressed completely except for that swollen rod of pleasure. "I'll do it. I'll scream at the top of my lungs."

He let out my favorite chuckle, the one that vibrated low in his throat and made a shiver roll through my body. "Go ahead. You think anyone can hear us up here? They can't."

Clutching the torso of my dress with both hands, he pulled in opposite directions, tearing the fabric at the buttons, and exposing the lacy red bra I'd bought for the holiday.

I hadn't imagined it would be revealed quite like this. Obviously, I needed a better imagination because this was the best way to show off the new item.

His eyes glazed as he traced over my spiked nipples through the material. It was too gentle of a touch that had me writhing and shaking. Pure torture of the best kind.

When he roughly pulled down the cups of the bra so he could palm my breasts, I screamed. Loud and with gusto.

I couldn't yell like that at our apartment. Someone would actually come to help, but he was right about no one being able to hear us at the office—the security guards were stationed too far away and wouldn't come to the floor unless the alarm went off—and though my insides were shouting something more like *Holy hell I am so turned on right now*, the words that I let out were, "Help me! Somebody help me!"

He pinched my nipples hard in reply, prompting my back to arch up. I let out another scream.

"No one will hear you, but that's definitely annoying," he said after several seconds of shrill howling. "Good thing I know just how to shut you up."

He crawled up my body until he was sitting over my face, the head of his cock poised at my lips. "Suck it," he said. "No teeth or you'll regret it."

My mouth watered, wanting him. But I forced my lips together in refusal.

"Open your mouth and suck it." He was more demanding this time, the intensity making my pussy clench in awe.

Still, I shook my head and kept my mouth shut tight.

Swiftly, he climbed off of me. Still on his knees, he dragged me to the front of Ellen's desk. He sat there, his back against the desk with his legs spread apart so that he could maneuver me in between them. In this position, he had full control of my head. One sharp pull of my hair, and my mouth fell open on a yelp, cutting off as he shoved his cock forcefully between my lips.

"We could have done this the easy way," he said as he forced my head up and down over him. "I'm very happy you chose this way instead."

Despite the sting at my scalp and not being able to catch a full breath, I was too. He'd never fucked my mouth so aggressively, his tip hitting the back of my throat on each stroke, sometimes reaching farther when he pushed his hips up so I would take him deep. My eyes began to water. I gagged more than once. Several times. I was suddenly grateful that I hadn't found anything to eat in the kitchen because I wasn't sure I would have been able to keep it down.

And still, I was pretty sure I was as close to orgasm as he was.

"I knew your mouth was good for something besides squealing." His words came out in breathy grunts. "Does your cunt feel as tight as your throat? Should we find out?"

I moaned, a muffled sound that could have been a cry of protest or a cry of longing. He shuddered as the sound vibrated over his cock, causing him to abruptly pull out.

"I'll take that as a yes. But if it was a no, that's fun too." He stood, and when I refused to stand with him, he picked me up and laid me on top of Ellen's desk.

I kicked and thrashed, but that only caused my dress to rip more as he worked his hands up my skirt. The lace thong I'd worn was even easier for him to get through, coming apart with one hard yank. He took a moment to sniff them, the erotic sight making me more aroused before he stuffed the flimsy ball of material in my mouth.

I lifted my head to spit them out, but he was quicker. He shoved my head back down with one hand while the other pulled a strip of tape off Ellen's dispenser. He placed two over my mouth to hold the panties in, then, with his hands gripping my hips, he pulled me to the edge of the desk and positioned himself at my weeping pussy.

Greediness bloomed inside me. My body throbbed with the anticipation of his cock, and still, I doled out one last attempt to resist, knowing that the longer I fought him off, the more glorious his intrusion would be. My knees pressed tight together, I pushed at his chest with the heels of my feet, my shoes lost earlier in our struggle.

It was a valiant effort, earning me a primal roar that seemed to originate from deep inside Donovan as he pushed my knees apart with his elbows. Then, grabbing my ankles and bending my legs into my chest so that I couldn't wield them as weapons, he once again notched his cock at my entrance and drove all the way in with one solid thrust.

The foreplay was over. He'd reached his destination, and now the fucking would begin.

FOUR

AS SOON AS he was inside me, my body exploded in pleasure. The orgasm had built as we'd wrestled, building further when he'd torn my dress, further still when he'd fucked my mouth. Each section of our play escalating my arousal like movements in a triumphant symphony, and now, at the climax, I surrendered to the beauty of the song.

Rainbowed stars sparked in front of my eyes as I convulsed, every part of me lit up with bliss. Was there any higher ecstasy than this? Than being at the receiving end of Donovan's wicked, hammering brutality? If there was, I didn't care to know. There was no other kind of love I wanted to encounter than his.

When my vision cleared, I looked up at him in a daze. He was a portrait of stunning vulgarity—a masked man taking whatever he pleased, using my body in whatever way he saw fit. My arms ached from their wrenched position behind my back, the discomfort a satisfactory addition to the lewdity. As he battered into me in steady rhythmic jabs, the sound of our thighs slapped underscoring the erotic scene.

Another climax stirred, slowly. Too slowly.

In frustration, I began to squirm, needing more, needing something. Needing, needing, needing. My hands wriggled against their binding, and with enough twisting and jerking, they got free. I pulled them from behind me, and reached one up for Donovan's mask, wanting it gone, wanting to see his face contort with his exertion.

As soon as it was in the air, though, he caught it. He seized the other as well and pinned them over my head, pressing his body inward to hold my legs down with his chest.

The shift in position opened me up wider and now his pelvis hit against my clit, the friction giving me just what I needed. My orgasm undulated through me in gaping ripples, each wave yawning with ecstasy that made my breath hitch and my skin burn.

"Fuck," Donovan grunted as I clamped down on his cock. "You tried to not want this, but your cunt has me gripped like it never wants to let me go. Such a filthy, greedy girl, aren't you?"

His cock twitched inside me, his thrusts slowed. Then he grated out a low rumble, his hips stuttering against my pussy as he emptied himself inside me. Long seconds passed before he'd finished coming. When he was finally done, he collapsed on top of me, his chest heaving in near rhythm with mine.

When he'd caught his breath, he stood and pulled me to a sitting position so he could remove the tape and panties from my mouth. He took off his mask next and then cradled my face in his hands. "How are you?"

"Really, really good." My body felt limp, but it hummed and tingled in complete satiation.

He studied my features, as if he wasn't ready to accept my answer until he'd done his own inspection. Satisfied with his findings, he smiled. "Good. Me too."

He leaned in, his lips skimming against mine once before he took full possession of my mouth, his tongue tasting me in deep, proprietary licks. I opened up completely for him, letting him take my mouth as aggressively as he'd taken my cunt. Wrapping one arm around his neck and another in his sweater, I pulled myself closer, wanting to show my gratitude as explicitly as possible.

It was a pretty thorough make-out session, and my lips were swollen and numb when he reluctantly broke away. "You're making me hard again."

"Is that a problem?"

"Considering the cleaning crew will be here soon? Yes."

"Ah. Good point." I forced my hands to release him, and sat back to watch as he tucked himself away. "Quite an untraditional Valentine's Day gift."

"Are you complaining?"

"I am not."

"I am glad." His grin made me woozy. "But it wasn't really a Valentine's Day gift."

My brows tilted inward. "It wasn't?"

He scanned the room. "I've been wanting to do this for you," he said, retrieving a glove off the floor. "And when I realized this morning that I was going to be in the doghouse if I didn't do something today, I decided to make it happen."

The tension that had been released from orgasming returned to settle in my jaw. His remark wasn't exactly off-putting, yet somehow it felt like a deliberate jab at me. I tried to keep a civil tone, but in the end I bristled. "Not a fan of February 14th?"

He looked up at me, his expression flecked with guilt. "I'm a fan of you."

I pursed my lips, not sure why I was upset. He'd given me a gift, whether he said it was for the holiday or not, a gift I enjoyed very much. He was into me. He was here. Why did it matter if he wasn't quite the romantic knight?

I must have been easy to read because his eyes did the thing they did when he was annoyed with me—not quite an eye roll, but close.

Then he sighed. "Look, Sabrina," he said, his expression stern. "Valentine's Day is a bullshit holiday. It's about money and proving your place in a cultural structure that you and I already know we exist outside of. You think a dozen roses and a tennis bracelet will validate our relationship? You think if I take you out to a romantic dinner that it will sufficiently express the emotions I have for you?"

He stepped closer to the desk, leaning his hands on either side of me to cage me in. "I'm in love with you. If you need to hear it, I can tell you again. But I don't think those words can be any clearer than my actions. I've lived the last ten years for you. I made you move into my home. Certainly that tells you more about my feelings than a box of chocolates could.

"So don't fuss about the shit I didn't do for you today—"

I'd been melting, but at this I had to protest. "I didn't—"

He cut me off. "—And look at what I do for you *every* day. Nationally certified occasion or not."

My frown lingered. Donovan made me weak, and I hated to give in easily. But I had no ground to stand on. I didn't need stupid holidays to tell me how he felt. What he'd said was perfect, and *he* was perfect, and I couldn't resist loving every unconventional bone in his body.

I reached my hand up to caress against his stubbled jaw. "Say it again."

He paused briefly, possibly to be sure he knew what I was asking. Then his arms came around my waist. "I love you," he said. "I really love you, might be more accurate. I live-my-life-around-you love you is better still."

I stretched both arms up to wrap around his neck. "I live-my-life-around-you love you too."

His lips twitched. He couldn't help himself, he had to say it. "But I've done it longer."

"It's not a competition," I laughed.

"It's not? Because I'm pretty sure I won." He gave me a quick kiss then swatted my hip. "Come on. Get dressed. I have a change of clothes for both of us in the stairwell. I didn't bring any panties, though." He swiped the thong from the desk and held it up. "And I'm keeping these."

He tucked his prize in his pocket then helped me off of the desk.

"Are we going somewhere?" I asked. My stomach growled loudly, as though wanting a say in our after-fucking plans.

Donovan raised a brow at the intrusion. "Okazu. It's not a date because it's Valentine's Day. It's a date because I'm hungry, and I always like feasting on you best."

Okazu was our favorite Japanese restaurant. The private rooms and low-to-the-ground tables made it easy to fool around in the filthiest ways. We'd taken full advantage in the past, and I had a pretty good feeling tonight would be no different.

"Sounds awesome. I'm obviously starving."

"Not surprising since you didn't eat."

I smiled guiltily. "You know me so well."

Together we cleaned up Ellen's desk, putting the phone back in its place and straightening the items we'd knocked over while fucking. I hadn't realized we'd been so destructive. It made me hot to see the remains.

When we were finished, I wiped some of her Purell over her desk. It probably wasn't very professional to have sex on your secretary's desk, even if she'd never know. The least I could do was leave it sanitized.

"I'll grab the clothes while you're shutting down your office. I need to stop by my office too, to erase the security recording."

Damn. I'd forgotten about the cameras. Thank God Donovan always thought of everything. I could just imagine one of the partners accidentally watching what we'd done.

"Wait," I said, stopping him before he'd left. "Can you maybe make a copy for us first?"

He grinned. "There's already a duplicate feed running to the apartment."

"Of course there is." I wasn't always happy about Donovan's penchant for surveillance, but this time I had to admit I saw the benefit. "We should watch it as soon as we get home."

His expression was serious, but he crossed back to me in two swift steps, swooping me once again into his arms for a slow, passionate kiss. When he broke away, he whispered in my ear. "Mamoritai. Daiji ni Shitai. Aishiteru."

I didn't speak Japanese, but he'd said these words to me enough times now that I knew what they meant. *I want to protect you. I treasure you. I love you.* There was nothing more I needed from a man than to be protected, treasured, and loved.

I'd been foolish earlier, when I'd thought we didn't speak the same love language. Obviously we did, because time and time again Donovan had proven all three sentiments to me. Proven that he could protect me. Proven that he treasured me. Proven that he loved me. Sometimes in the dirtiest, filthiest ways.

But always in the richest ways too.

**Donovan and Sabrina first appear in the
Dirty Duet.
Start with Dirty Filthy Rich Boys which is
available everywhere for FREE.**

FILTHY VALENTINE FIX

ONE

"THE FINANCIAL REPORTS you signed off on have been delivered to Ms. Anders-Sitkin. I rescheduled your Monday afternoon like you asked, and here's the proposal from the new tech company you're looking into. I had it bound so you can read it over the weekend." It was Friday just after four, and I was giving my boss my report before he left for the day.

When I first started working for Hudson Pierce, I'd always been the one to leave first. A man didn't get as successful as he did without being a workaholic, and he definitely was one. After he got married six years ago, however, he became more balanced and started leaving at the same time I did. The birth of his twins seven months ago changed his habits once again, and now he occasionally left before me, especially since his wife began displaying signs of postpartum OCD.

"Good, good. That's all good." He took the report I handed him and stuffed it into his briefcase without looking at it, seemingly preoccupied. He was in a hurry to get out of there, I could tell, his eyes darting between his watch and the elevator.

"Just one more thing. You had a delivery from Cartier." I unlocked the bottom drawer where I had stashed the long box when it had come in by courier, assuming whatever was inside was most likely valuable.

Hudson perked up at this. "Oh. I've been waiting for this." The stoic man appeared almost excited as he took the box from me and opened it, the lid blocking my view of the contents. "Have you looked?"

"Of course not, Mr. Pierce." I was appalled. As if I wasn't an absolute professional. I took my job as his secretary with pride.

It was in other areas of my life that I was naughty.

He turned the box so I could see the necklace. It was simple but breathtaking, a plain opal stone enclosed between two rubies. "It's magnificent," I said, imagining it cost more than my monthly salary. "They're the birthstones of your children, aren't they?"

"Yes. Opals are Mina's and the rubies are the twins'." His voice was filled with pride. I planned never to have children, but if anyone came close to convincing me that the thought wasn't completely abhorrent, it was Hudson.

"Mrs. Pierce will love that. A truly thoughtful gift. Any special occasion?" The man never needed a reason to give his wife gifts, but this one was above and beyond.

Though, maybe the occasion this time was that her mental health was suffering. I regretted asking as soon as the thought occurred to me.

He looked at me as if I'd forgotten something important. "Valentine's Day."

Oh, fuck. I had forgotten something important. "Is that coming up already?"

"It's next Wednesday. I'm surprised it isn't on your mind since you have a boyfriend."

Yeah, that was surprising. For entirely different reasons than he was suggesting.

I straightened the tape dispenser and the Kleenex box on my desk even though they were already perfectly straight. "Nate isn't really my boyfriend," I said, not knowing how to explain to him—or anyone—what my relationship with Nate was. It was definitely something I didn't like to discuss with my boss. The only reason Hudson knew I was seeing the Creative Director of the ad firm he used was because we'd bumped into each other at a wedding. "We're, uh, neighbors. Neighbors that get along really well."

Actually, we were only neighbors *because* we got along really well. He'd rented the apartment next door just to be close to me. And by *get along really well*, what I meant was had *lots of kinky sex.*

That wasn't fair. Nate and I were more than just fuck-buddies. I had feelings for him that were difficult to pin down, mostly because I was a woman who never wanted to be pinned down at all. Fortunately, he understood because he was exactly the same.

Or, at least, he *said* he was. In the two months since we'd become "neighbors," we'd seemed to be on the same page. We saw each other most days, but it wasn't a big deal when we didn't. We enjoyed our time together without being overly clingy. We didn't talk too much about our emotions, except when absolutely necessary. We continued to attend The Open Door, the weekly sex party that we'd first met at, and though we always came and left together, we still fooled around with a wide variety of people while we were there.

Honestly, I was living my best life.

But now that Valentine's Day was here, I had my doubts. This was the holiday that brought out the romantic of even the most laid-back lovers. The holiday that incited declarations of devotion and inspired conversations about commitment. While mainly a place of debauchery and overindulgence of the sexual kind, the Open Door even had a ceremony the Saturday prior to Valentine's Day that allowed lovers to proclaim their feelings vocally along with physically.

If Nate was ever going to ruin our "neighbor" status with talk of love, this would be when he'd do it.

"You never know what neighbors can turn into," Hudson said, assuming that I wanted encouragement. "Alayna was once my employee, remember."

"Right. Thank you." This conversation needed to be ended in whatever means possible. "Well, Mrs. Pierce is going to love your gift. Is there anything else you need from me on your way out?"

"No. Thank you, Patricia. That will be all. Enjoy your weekend."

"You too," I said, smiling despite the dread gathering in my stomach. Weekends were what I lived for. Specifically, Saturday nights at the Open Door. Nate and I very rarely missed a party.

This Saturday, however, the Saturday before Valentine's Day, I was going to have to think of a clever way to get us out of it.

TWO

THE PROBLEM with getting out of going to the Open Door was that I'd have to tell Nate *why* I didn't want to go. And that in itself meant talking about feelings, which was something I tried to avoid at all costs.

So rather than say anything, I let it fester. When he knocked on my door that evening with takeout in hand, I invited him in, but as soon as the food was gone (which was after he'd fucked me against the refrigerator), I told him I needed some alone time, and he left without any fuss.

That didn't seem like the behavior of a man on the verge of spilling his romantic guts. So when it was time to get ready for the party Saturday night, I almost went on with the routine as usual.

Then, when I was in my closet trying to choose a dress, all I could think about was, *which outfit did I want to be wearing when Nate ruined everything?* A stupid question considering the fact that I'd likely be naked by that point.

Even more stupid because if I was really worried he was going to ruin everything, then why would I let it happen?

I was halfway out the door on my way to his when I realized that canceling was just as problematic. If I told him I was sick, he'd offer to stay home and take care of me. And if he had intentions of pouring out his heart, he'd potentially do it then. Being alone when that happened was a worse thought than being in the midst of friends.

Alternatively, I could tell him I was too sick for company. But then he might wait until Valentine's Day to deliver the bomb. If I got out of seeing him that night, he'd get to me eventually, unless I planned to avoid him forever, which...was that a possibility? Could I just keep giving him the slip? Ghost him and end things like that?

If he didn't live next door, maybe.

Besides, I didn't *want* to ghost him. I didn't want to lose him. I wanted to keep things exactly like they were, which meant I should act like I always did and go to the party as usual.

I was still in my doorway mulling it over when the man I was mulling came walking down the hall from the direction of the elevator, recyclable grocery bag in hand.

"Hey, babe. You looking for me?"

I wrapped my robe tighter around me, feeling naked in a way that had nothing to do with my body. "Uh...no."

He quirked a brow. "Just like to stand in the hallway in your bathrobe? I can get behind that, but I gotta say I'm a little jealous I wasn't invited to the party."

He was joking, but he also wasn't. He would have zero problem with me entertaining strangers in whatever kinky way I wished, but he preferred that if I did, he'd get to watch.

I preferred that too. It was what I loved about our arrangement. I still got to play in every dirty, filthy way I'd come to enjoy, *and* I got to have him be a part of it. Like I said —living my best life.

But I wasn't in the hallway for kink, and I needed to make a decision once and for all about the night. "I mean I was coming to tell you that I didn't know if I was up to going tonight, then I changed my mind."

His green eyes narrowed in on me. "You feeling okay?"

Ugh. Now he was concerned. "Yes. No. I don't know. Just a bit tired, I guess."

"It's not like you to want to skip out on a party for being tired."

"I know, right? Which is why I changed my mind."

"Are you sure? We could stay in. Order bone broth from that place you like down the street."

Just like I'd predicted, he'd want to take care of me. "I'm sure. I just needed to get up and walk around to get my pep back. Give me an hour to primp."

"I'll give you two."

God, he knew me so well.

Two hours later, I was dressed in a black mesh maxi, high slits that came up to my hips on both sides. (I rarely wore underwear to these parties, and I didn't this time either— made for easier access and less items to keep track of when it was time to go home.) My hair was down in curls, my face made-up. With my fake lashes, bright red lipstick, slip-off heels, and a trench coat so that I wouldn't be arrested for indecency, I was ready to go when Nate knocked.

I crossed to the door and paused, my stomach fluttering all of a sudden. I liked this guy so much. So much. I might even go so far as to say another L word about my feelings, if I actually took the time to name them. I didn't want to lose what we had, and if that meant putting on my big-girl panties —or, in this case, putting on panties at all—then I needed to do that and nip any problems in the bud.

He rapped again, just as I opened the door. "Hey, you."

He was dazzling in his tux and motorcycle jacket, both hardcore and opulence at once. He raised a hand to rub over his close-trimmed beard and dragged his eyes down my body. "Well, hello yourself."

I looked down to realize my coat was still open, giving him a peek at the goods underneath. Glowing from the heat in his gaze, I tied the belt around my waist. "That's for later, big boy. If you're good."

"I can be very, very good."

He could also be very, very bad, thoughts of which made my pussy clench in anticipation.

Except, if I wanted there to be something to actually look forward to later, I needed to say some things now. I gestured to my apartment. "Can we talk a minute before we go?"

He frowned and looked at his cell phone. "The Lyft is already downstairs. Can we talk in the car?"

I bit my lip, fretting. Talking in the car meant there'd be no escape if the conversation went wrong. I tried never to have heavy conversations without an escape route.

"Hey," Nate said, stepping closer so he could put an anchoring hand on my hip. "I know what you're worrying about."

"You do?" He couldn't possibly, but I was highly curious about whatever it was he *thought* I was concerned about.

"Yes. I do, and I'm telling you right now you don't need to. I know what we are."

My breath hitched. Maybe he really did know what I was worried about, and if so, it sure sounded like he wasn't going to make a big display tonight after all.

Which was good. I was relieved.

"Awesome. Then, let's go." Of course, there was always a chance that we weren't on the same page, that he was referring to something else altogether, but asking to clarify would mean talking more about it, and if I didn't *have* to talk more about it...

Well, it was obvious which option I was going to take.

THREE

SAFETY WAS the number one concern at the Open Door. There were several measures taken to ensure that everyone who attended was unharmed during the fun. A password was required for entrance, a new one was given each week. Phones and wallets were turned in at the door. Condoms were always available throughout the space, and consent was emphatically emphasized.

One way consent was emphasized was by the wearing of different colored bracelets that party-goers picked up at the front door. Everyone was required to don one. White meant the wearer preferred to initiate interaction. Black meant that verbal consent was required before anyone touched or complimented the wearer. Red meant that physical compliments and non-sexual touch were welcomed as a means of initiation. If anyone was caught not following the rules of the bracelet, the offender was banned for life.

The only exception was during official games. In those

cases, those who played gave consent to allow sexual touch as part of the game without specifically verbalizing it. So when playing naked Twister, a person didn't have to ask for consent from the people they tangled with when putting an elbow on yellow and a foot on blue.

However.

Some of the kinkier attendees preferred their consent to be more dubious throughout the parties, not just during game play. While not exactly supported by the club administration, those in the know would often wear a bronze bracelet as well as a red. Bronze meant *If you touch me sexually without asking first, I might tell you no thank you, but I'm not gonna be mad.*

I was one of those who wore a bronze bracelet.

That didn't mean I didn't have rules, because I did. I always wore a mask to hide my identity—too many people knew Hudson Pierce, and I did not mix business with pleasure. I never gave my name—people referred to me only as T or Mistress T or Madame T or some other variation. And, while I welcomed all sorts of fingers and mouths and toys in my pussy, I did not allow any penetration with a cock.

I'd broken all those rules with Nate, of course, but that was what kept our relationship special. No matter how much I fooled around with others, there were parts of my body that I only shared with him.

Was that love?

Maybe.

It didn't mean I thought we should be making declarations about it. The arrangement itself was enough to make it significant. We didn't need labels or any other words to distinguish it, and if Nate really was the perfect guy for me, he would understand that as well as I did.

I just didn't know for sure that he did.

So after we'd checked in and the host for the evening—a non-binary Puerto Rican with luscious lips and gorgeous brown skin—informed us that the Valentine's Day devotions were being held in the great room to the left, I immediately tugged Nate in the opposite direction.

"Hold up," he said, when I'd taken several steps. "Is there somewhere specific you're headed?"

I opened my mouth, my mind racing to come up with something on the spot. I'd stopped listening to the host, though, the minute they said where the devotions were, and I had no idea what else was happening around the penthouse.

"Nowhere specific," I said lamely after several awkward seconds. *Just somewhere far, far away from the "lovey-dovey" room.*

"Do you mind if I take the lead, then?"

Nate never asked to take the lead. He was a go-with-the-flow kind of guy, and usually the flow went wherever I wanted to be.

He definitely had something planned.

My stomach felt like lead. What was I supposed to say? How could I tell him no when he had asked so little of me?

"Yeah. Sure." I feigned a smile as I followed him back toward the great room, a tightness spreading across my ribs as though I were wearing a corset versus no underwear at all.

But Nate didn't stop in the great room. Instead, he led me along the wall, avoiding the circle where devotions were already being declared. As much as they made me uncomfortable, I was intrigued by those who enjoyed spouting their emotions to a room full of strangers, so I scanned the audience as we passed by. Some were recognizable from previous parties, others from work. The host of a famous podcast with his boyfriend. A state representative from the political party I didn't vote for. A British media mogul who partnered with Hudson, along with his wife, another old acquaintance of my boss.

Before I could spot anyone else I knew, we were out of the room and in the library.

Well. This was unexpected.

Not that I was complaining.

The vibe here was much more my style. The lights were low, people were in various states of undress, and sexual play was well underway. A woman I knew as Justice had another woman I didn't know bent over a spanking bench. A swing hung from four chains in the ceiling, empty, but in motion as though it had been recently used. Andrew was pinching the nipples of a distinguished gentleman who was riding the Sybian saddle. Lots of people I knew were here, many bronze bracelets visible.

Yes. This was an excellent choice indeed.

Kennedy looked up from the pussy he was pleasuring with his fingers. "Mistress T. Want to come play?" He gestured down to the tent in his pants. It was a cock I knew well, a little on the short side, but thick and pretty. One I enjoyed putting down my throat.

I glanced at Nate—not for permission, just because my eyes naturally went to him when he was in a room—and saw he'd already found a seat at the edge of the room, in the shadows but with a great view. Knowing his gaze would be pinned to me, I gathered the skirt of my dress in my hands and knelt in front of the couch where he was seated and worked on getting Kennedy's gorgeous cock free.

After a fair amount of teasing, I'd just put my lips around his crown when someone cleared his throat behind me.

"On this Saturday before Valentine's Day," the familiar voice said. "I'd like to make a declaration of my devotion."

Ah, fuck.

It wasn't Nate speaking, which was a good thing, but if the activity in this room was going to turn into devotions, how long before he joined in?

I decided to ignore it. Pretend Chuck Richard wasn't speaking at all. That the mood wasn't being ruined at all. Though, as I resumed sucking Kennedy into my mouth, I wondered who the hell Chuck would make a declaration about. He'd never paired off with any one individual at a party before. Most times I saw him, he spent the evening trying to get me to go home with him.

Curiosity forbid my ears from tuning out.

"I know these declarations are usually made with words, but I believe this one would be best appreciated in action." A beat passed. "Mistress T?"

I choked, and not just because I had a cock down my throat. "Um," I said, gliding off the dick. It fell out of my mouth with a pop as I looked toward Chuck. "Me?"

He nodded.

I shot a glance at Nate. He'd unbuttoned his jacket and loosened his tie, but didn't seem either shocked or bothered by the turn in events.

He was watching though. Watching *me*. As he always was.

I peered up at Kennedy next who simply shrugged. Not

sure how to handle Chuck's out-of-the-blue declaration, I at least knew I couldn't ignore it entirely. That would cause more of a scene than responding.

I stood. "Chuck, I..."

"Come here, please," he said, dismissing my unfinished statement. Cautiously, I stepped toward him. When I was close enough, he took my elbow and tugged me toward the swing. Then he gathered my dress for me up around my waist and handed it to me to hold so he could lift me up into the seat.

Okay.

Chuck was always into kink, but he wasn't usually the one who took the lead on anything. This was definitely new and different.

And being someone who liked new and different, especially where sexual activities were concerned, it was something I could go along with, however out of the ordinary it was.

With expertise, Chuck situated me in the swing, propping my feet up in the stirrups so my knees were bent and spread, the mesh material of my dress draped to the side and out of the way. When he moved behind me to secure my hands behind my head, I saw that I was positioned to have the perfect view of Nate.

Or, rather, Nate had the perfect view of *me*, my thighs opened wide, my most private parts revealed and facing him as though I'd been posed for his enjoyment.

I was instantly wet.

I met his eyes, wondering, could he tell? Could he see the glistening on my bare skin? Could he see that I was dripping?

I spent every Saturday night naked at these parties. I'd rarely felt quite so exposed. Rarely felt quite so vulnerable.

My breath shuddered with the realization.

Then Chuck's hands came around the swing to capture my breasts through my dress, and my gaze broke from Nate's as my head fell back in ecstasy.

FOUR

LOST in the enjoyment of Chuck's breast play, I didn't notice that Justice had finished up with her spanking session.

"On this Saturday before Valentine's Day, I also have a declaration," she said. "One better shown than spoken."

Justice too? What the hell?

When I lifted my head to look, she was on the ground crawling toward me, her naked full breasts bouncing as she moved across the floor. Chuck eased up on the nipple play as we both stared.

Then Justice was between my legs, her hands sweeping down my inner thighs before settling on my pussy. Here, her thumbs traced my slit, one going up to lift the skin hiding my clit, the other going lower, lower still. Using my own juices as lube, she slid the digit into my back entrance as her mouth lowered to suck the swollen bundle of nerves.

"Holy shit," I cried out, feeling an orgasm begin to churn deep inside me. Justice was a pussy-licking goddess. Who knew? I certainly didn't. I'd had my face between her thighs plenty of times myself, and been spanked by her a few times as well, but she wasn't a domme who was very generous with giving out pleasure. Which was fine—she doled out punishment with mastery. I'd never wanted anything more from her.

Turned out she was a woman of many skills. How fortunate was I?

While Justice feasted, Chuck did as well, moving to kneel at my side so he could suck on my breasts as well as play with them. At first, he adored them through the material of my dress, but soon he pushed my dress up higher so he could lick and suck my bare skin.

I came as soon as he used his teeth.

It was then that Kennedy made his declaration. "On this Saturday before Valentine's Day..." He trailed off. "Hell, you know the spiel by now."

He came around behind me and wrapped his hand in my hair. With a sharp yank, he tugged my head back. Then he bent down and began to kiss me, his nose pressing against my chin, his tongue plundering deep into my mouth. He kissed me and kissed me, one hand holding my head where he wanted it, the other reaching up to fondle the breast that Chuck was neglecting.

And as I surrendered to the abundance of pleasure, with so many mouths and hands and tongues and teeth all focused on me, I was still clearly aware of Nate across the room, watching me, probably holding his cock at this point. My eyes were closed, but I could picture him stroking himself, could picture him getting off on my enjoyment, and with sudden distinct clarity, I knew that he was behind this. That this pleasure orgy centered on me was all him.

The realization sent another full-blown orgasm ricocheting through my body, turning my skin into fire and making my body shake with the intensity.

Kennedy released my mouth so I could properly vocalize my rapture, so when I'd settled and the spots had cleared from my eyes, I could see that Nate was no longer across the room, but standing at my side, opposite Chuck. His cock was indeed out, his fist pumping swiftly up and down the length, his face scrunched up in that expression that said he was about to come.

With a jagged moan, he released, spilling his cum over my chest in hot white ribbons. It was hot and it was kinky and so many men had come on me at these parties without it meaning anything, but I had no doubt that this particular marking was all about claiming me as his.

And, to my surprise, I didn't mind.

I didn't only not mind, it thrilled me.

Suddenly needing to stand, I thrashed against my restraints. "Help me up?" I said to no one specific.

Kennedy moved to undo my hands while Justice and Chuck released my feet. Nate grabbed a wet wipe and cleaned me off and was done and had retreated back to the side by the time I was free and standing again.

"Thank you, guys. Kennedy, Justice, Chuck. I'll pay you all back, I swear." But right now I had other priorities.

I crossed to Nate and, grabbing him by the lapels, I yanked him into me. My mouth crashed against his, devouring him like a sex-starved woman rather than a woman who had just gotten off multiple times in a crowd.

When our kiss had progressed to the point that we needed to either cut it off or move to a prone position, I pulled away, and, without taking even a second to think about it, I said the words I never thought I'd tell a man, especially not in public. "I love you."

Nate's eyes went wide. He shook his head in surprise. "Whoa."

Heat spread across my face, and I was a girl who only ever flushed during sexual activities, never from embarrassment. "I mean...I didn't mean...I shouldn't have..." Fuck.

Fuck, fuck, fuck.

Nate cupped a large hand around my face. "Hey. It's all good. You surprised me is all. I love you, too."

I drew in a breath and blinked back whatever was happening in my tear ducts. "It is good, isn't it? This is good. It's all good."

He chuckled. "Yeah. I think it is. We're good."

"I love you, and we're good." Geez, now I couldn't stop saying it.

He nodded, his face growing solemn. "I love you, and we're good."

He kissed me again, slower this time, his lips reassuring me, his tongue tethering me then releasing me again. It mirrored the way we were together, two balloons soaring in the sky, tied together at the strings, pulling away and coming back together, over and over in the wind.

He pulled away this time. With a swat on my ass, he nudged me back toward the others. "You owe some people some paybacks. Go play. Give me a show."

Later, it would be just me and him, in this room, maybe, or in a bedroom upstairs or back at one of our apartments. We'd be naked together, our skin pressing everywhere, as he fucked me, his measured thrusts taking me to places I could never reach with anyone but him.

But for now, he would watch.

And I would play, sure in his love and certain that he'd always be there for me when I returned.

Read more about Trish and Nate and their adventures at the Open Door in Dirty Filthy Fix, a 1001 Dark Nights novella.

For more stories featuring the Open Door, check out these titles:
The Open Door, a 1001 Dark Nights novella
and
Rivalry

DIRTY SWEET VALENTINE

DIRTY SWEET VALENTINE

I'd imagined Harrington Steele on my doorstep countless times.

How he looked varied in my fantasies over the years, changing based on trends and the current whims of my heart. Sometimes the stubbled jaw that I'd loved so much became a full beard. Sometimes the lines by his mouth had deepened. Sometimes he wore a fitted suit like he'd donned that night we saw *Carmen* at the opera. Most times he wore a pair of jeans and a Henley, the look I remember on him most. Sometimes he'd changed so much I barely recognized him, and I had to squint and ask in an unsteady voice, "Harrington?"

Sometimes I knew him immediately, but pretended I didn't. I fancied it gave me somewhat of an upper hand to play ignorant. To play detached and unaffected. Showing him that I had been just fine without him, that he hadn't altered my very DNA by leaving and taking my heart with him.

And sometimes there were no games, no pretenses, only jubilation. Only pure bliss. Those times I fell silently into his arms and kissed him with all the emotions I'd kept pent up since he'd said goodbye that winter evening one and a half decades ago.

Nothing I'd imagined, however, compares to the reality. Nothing I'd imagined prepared me in the least, and after opening the door and finding him here in the flesh—on Valentine's Day, no less—the most prevalent emotion inside me is relief.

Relief because I always knew he'd come back. Relief because I can finally stop waiting, stop questioning, stop wondering *when*. Relief because I can set down this weight of longing I've carried for so long, roll my shoulders back, and stand tall like the strong woman I've been pretending I am.

I did know him immediately. Of course I did. There wasn't even a second's pause before recognition. Even with the new creases by his eyes. Even with the receding hairline. He's still ruggedly handsome and devastatingly perfect. He's still my Harrington, and he still destroys me with a single glance. My knees have lost their steadiness. My breathing stutters as my chest rises and falls. My heart gallops away from me, and if he keeps studying me the way I'm studying him, like I'm a precious jewel that he's spent his lifetime searching for, then I'm going to collapse in a heap at his feet.

"Amelia," he says roughly, and I'm practically undone. I thought I'd remembered exactly how sweet the word sounds on his tongue, but I was wrong. I'd forgotten it was this delicious. Forgotten how he can make four simple syllables sound like a prayer. How he can make me feel not just loved but revered. As though it were the name of a saint instead of plain old boring me.

Plain old boring me has yet to speak. Years of fantasizing about this, and I don't have a single word at the ready. There are too many questions, too much history to sum up in a simple greeting. All I know is that when I do find a way to articulate the things I want to say, I don't want to speak them on the threshold with the cold blustering in around us.

I reach out and wrap my hand in his plaid wool coat and tug him inside my flat.

Face to face in my entry isn't necessarily any better. Here I catch his oak scent, as familiar as if he'd just walked out yesterday. It triggers my muscle memory, and before I can catch myself, my fingers are floating toward his face to scratch along the scruff of his jaw the way I did so many times back then.

I stop just in time and let my hand fall to my side, even though I'm dying to touch him. Dying to be sure he's real. That it wasn't a ghost that turned up on my step after all—a very real possibility. There's too much I need to know before I let myself get carried away, and if I touch him, I'm sure that's exactly what will happen. I'll be swept up in his current and lose sight of the shore before I realize I don't have a life jacket.

"Are you here for good?" It's the most important question, and somehow my mouth forms the words perfectly, shaping them into respectable dialogue.

His answer comes just as steady. "I'm here for tonight."

With that, the parameters have been set, and I immediately feel confined. I spin on my heel and head to my kitchen.

A plate with two slices of seven-grain bread sits on the worktop next to a plastic container of chicken salad, the sandwich deserted with the knock at the door. I ignore it again now, and standing on tiptoes, I reach into the top of the cupboard where I keep the liquor. The hard liquor. I pull down a bottle of bourbon and a shot glass. When I turn around again, I see that Harrington has followed.

"Would you like one as well?" I offer. I'm already loosening the cap and filling my shot.

"I'm good, thank you."

I'm not. Not good. Not even close to good.

I throw the liquor back and savor the burn as it slides down my throat. It tastes like Harrington smells, comforting and masculine. Then I fill the shot again.

"You need another?"

Harrington was never judgmental when I knew him. Not of me, anyway, and his appraisal now gives me pause. Irritated pause. It's a little presumptuous for him to waltz in here after all this time and then cast aspersions.

I raise one eyebrow at him. "I've just seen a ghost. Forgive me for needing to steady my nerves."

Before I can bring the glass again to my lips, he grabs my wrist. The bourbon sloshes over the rim and onto my hand. His too, perhaps, but I can't bring myself to look anywhere other than at his face, at his cool blue irises. They're still as clear as they were the last time I stared into them. Still pools of tranquility, no matter what he may be feeling—or not feeling—inside.

"I didn't come back to fight you off of me, and I'm not fumbling around with you half-pissed, either." With his free hand, he takes the shot from me and sets it on the worktop.

I want to argue with the myriad assumptions in his statement, but I can't. He and I both know that I turn randy when inebriated. And as much as I'd like to take a bit more of the edge off, I'd regret it later if every detail of our night wasn't crystal clear in my memory.

He's brought us to an important question though. "Why *are* you here?"

"I had a meeting in London."

A meeting with *them*? I'm not allowed to ask because he's not allowed to answer. I already know more than I'm supposed to, and it's practically nothing. Harry was born in Wales, but since he lived most of his life in the U.S., I don't even know if the *them* he works for is here or there. I don't know if he's CIA or MI6. I don't know if he's James Bond or Ethan Hunt. Perhaps he's someone else entirely.

I scowl, hating the boundaries around me. I'm someone who likes to break through boundaries, through glass ceilings, through red tape and bureaucracy.

So fuck the rules. Fuck what I'm allowed. "You had a meeting? For...'work'?" I press in the same way I pressed back then, when I first found out about *them* to begin with.

"I had to see someone, yes," he clarifies without clearing anything up at all, but before I can push back, he says, "And I couldn't not see you, too."

His grip on me relaxes, but he doesn't let go. Instead, he turns my hand so my palm is face up. His thumb draws small circles on the inside of my wrist, and I dissolve into someone I haven't been in a long time—a woman happy in love.

Goosebumps sprout across my skin, and my pulse quickens. I know he can feel it through the thin skin he's touching, can feel exactly the effect he's always had on me.

"I can't stop looking at you now," he says, and I can barely breathe. "Can't stop touching you. I want to touch more of you."

My hand reaches up to brush a finger along his scruff like before, but this time I don't stop myself. My touch is tentative at first, then more confident as I bend my knuckles to stroke along his jaw.

He leans into my hand, and for one perfect second, nothing has changed.

"Amy," he says, his voice taut with restraint, bringing me back to the present. It's one word. Two simple syllables, but the underscore is clear—I'm the one who decides what happens next. The steering wheel is firmly in my hands.

One thing that hasn't changed in fifteen years—I still fail at self-preservation. Sure, I'm a single, self-made woman in the advertising world. A saleswoman that no man can rival. My colleagues respect me. I'm at the top of my game. I've risen above the racial prejudices leveled against me by my mixed Iranian/African/British heritage. I have an active sex life with no emotional attachments. Nothing hurts me. No one breaks my heart because I don't give anyone access to it.

But when it comes to Harrington—*Harry*—I'm defenseless.

It happens so fast, our coming together. Like it's automatic. I raise my chin and lean in, and that's all it takes before we meet, and his mouth is on mine, crushing me with his kiss. My lips move against his with an urgent desperation I've never known. It feels like grasping at sand. Like there's no way I can hold him, and even though my tongue is gliding against his and my hands are tangled in his hair, he's already slipping from my grip.

I'm frantic to clutch on, to seize as much of him as I can in the moment I have.

Never breaking the kiss, I slide my palms down his oh-my-God-still-so-firm chest to land at his belt. I fumble with the buckle as he pushes me back into the corner where the bar meets the worktop. My leg is already hitched up around his thigh when he lifts me onto the counter. He pushes my skirt up and shifts my panties aside so he can find the sensitive bud buried in the dark curls.

He smiles against my lips when he realizes how wet I already am. I'm not even sure when that happened—if I started drowning when he touched my wrist or when I first saw him on my doorstep, but I'm slick and slippery and he takes full advantage of it, rubbing my clit with his thumb while sliding his fingers along my drenched seam.

His touch is instantly familiar. These are his moves. If I were naked and blindfolded in a room of strangers, I'd still know this pressure, this pattern of swirls. My body remembers, and the knot of tension is quickly pulling taut, spiking pleasure across my core.

No one else has ever made me feel quite this way, something I had forgotten until he takes me there now.

Despite the distraction, I'm determined to feel the silk of his cock under my palm. I manage to get his trousers open, and I slip my hand under the elastic band of his boxers and wrap it around the thick steel I find underneath. It's an old friend, warm and solid in my grip. I slide my thumb across his head before tugging his length furiously. Punishingly. As though it's his cock that has me angry.

And I *am* angry. Maddeningly angry. I tell him with my kiss as well as my hands, biting at his lips, growling low in the back of my throat when he nips back. He stands his ground against me, bracing a firm palm behind my head to keep me in place while he continues to devour me with his mouth, while his other hand continues to wreak havoc on my nervous system.

His assault strengthens my strike against him. I increase the tempo of my handjob, determined to make him come first, or at least at the same time. I refuse to be weak and vulnerable alone. I've been weak and vulnerable alone for far too long.

I manage to hold my own in this war until he enters me with one long finger.

I gasp at the invasion, breaking away from his mouth to suck in the air I so desperately need. Harrington takes advantage of my lapse of control and brings out the big weapon—his filthy mouth. I've never been able to resist his dirty talk, and he knows it.

"Look how you swallow up my finger with your cunt," he says, his wicked eyes gleaming with pride. He presses his forehead to mine and crooks his equally wicked finger to massage against that spot—that fucking spot that only he has ever owned so precisely—and I immediately gush wetter.

"Yes, drench me, Amelia. Just like that. Show me what that pretty pussy is holding back. It belongs to me."

I'm still jerking his cock, but my hand stumbles noticeably in its stroke.

Harrington chuckles. "You know you can't win this battle, baby. Fall apart on me. Lose control."

It's the term of endearment that does me in—after all this time, after all these years, I'm still his baby. It doesn't matter that he might have said it without thinking or that he might have said it to countless women. I hear the naked honesty underscoring the simple word, and I shatter.

My body quivers, and spots form in front of my eyes. When they clear, he greets me with a smirk that tells me how much he enjoyed watching me come apart on his hand.

"Better now?" he asks as though his sexual charms are potent enough to fix everything that remains unspoken between us. Emphasizing his confidence, he sucks my juices off his finger.

Fifteen years older and Harrington Steele is still a cocky bastard. It's reassuring to know that there are some things in life that are constant.

Despite the renewed simmer of arousal in my belly, I roll my eyes and stare down at his abandoned cock, still hard and throbbing. My fingers close again around him, but he stops me. "Let that wait."

If we aren't going to fuck, then what does he want instead? He's still standing close, still caging me in. His gaze catches on my lips, and I suspect he'd be content to stay just like this—his hand stroking my arm, his lungs sharing the same air as mine.

It's extremely intimate. The kind of intimate that falls thick and heavy like the snow in the Alps. If I stay standing in its path, I'm likely to be crushed underneath the weight. Fucking would be easier. Fucking would be less intrusive.

But he's putting himself away, and I'm not in the mood to seduce him.

I push at him to move, then hop to the ground when he does. I head toward the bowl of chicken salad and the waiting slices of bread.

"I was just making supper. I assume you're staying?" It

isn't really a question. I pull out the loaf and reach for another plate from the cupboard even before he answers.

"I'm yours all night."

The comment smarts for complicated reasons. Because I've longed to be his for so long. Dreamed of it for all these years. Then, when I finally reclaim the title, it has a time limit attached.

I swipe at the sting like it's a pesky mosquito instead of the tightening of shackles that it feels like. I concentrate instead on my task, spooning the filling onto the bread, smooshing the slices together.

"Chicken salad's on the menu. Sorry. I know it's not your favorite." Not that I'd been expecting him. I hand him a plate, recognizing how pathetic it must seem that this was how I'd planned to spend my Valentine's Day evening. Frankly, I hate the holiday and choose to ignore it. It's perfectly normal to be alone on a Wednesday night after work. And a sandwich is perfectly suitable for a weekday dinner.

Still, I'm compelled to snatch a bottle of Chardonnay from the wine fridge to fancy the meal up.

A few minutes later, we're settled on the sofa in front of the fire. On the surface, it seems terribly romantic, but it's a gas-lit thing, only turned on with the flick of a switch, and I'd already had it going before my visitor arrived. The wine has been poured, though, and Harrington is sitting too close, his body turned in toward me. There's nowhere for me to move— I'm already seated against the arm. I consider asking him to back up and give me space, but, in the end, I like him this close as much as I don't.

We eat in thick silence, the kind of silence that's alive. It crawls along my skin and breathes heavily in my face, and everything, everything I want and need to say to this man hides in its shadow, gathering courage to step into the light. It's possible that I'm not that brave. Not that open to vulnerability.

"This is rather good," he says, halfway through his sandwich.

I chortle. "Please. You don't have to patronize me. I know you'd prefer corned beef or pastrami." He'd always liked his food "manly." Anything mixed with mayonnaise, and, god forbid, *grapes*, was immediately qualified as feminine.

"I'm as surprised as you are, but I'm quite serious." His brow knits as he considers the remaining half in his hand. He looks at it like I might look at a spreadsheet, determined to tease out the pertinent information. "Perhaps it's the pecans. I find the crunchy texture appealing."

I study his forehead as he talks, noting the new lines that mar the once smooth plane. I find *these* appealing. I long to trace them with my fingertips.

I also find them infuriating. Each groove is part of the story of his life, a life that has been lived longer without me than with. Stories he can never tell from a life I could never share.

My eyes sting suddenly, and I turn my head away. I feel him scrutinizing my profile, and I lose my appetite. I stack my plate on his and set it on the side table before concentrating on my wine, praying that the numbing effects of the alcohol take effect as soon as fucking possible.

It's not soon enough because I still feel too much when he sighs and says, "Oh, Amy, Amy. I'm dying to know what's going on behind those muddy eyes. Tell me some of it, won't you?"

My lids close briefly, an attempt to buffer the connection between us. It doesn't help. I still feel him reaching into me, sneaking under my skin with long, electric tentacles.

I clear my throat. I swallow. "Soraya passed," I say finally. "Three years ago now." My grandmother and I had been close, and Harry had known her well. We'd spent long hours at her studio, listening to her chatter in her broken English, watching as she painted her vibrant, abstract views of the world. She'd loved us together, loved the way we loved each other, and I was fairly certain she'd attempted to capture us in her broad-stroked art. The two had wound themselves together in my mind, and the joy in her paintings is always mingled with the want of him.

When she'd died, I'd wanted Harry desperately. I was sullen and sad and convinced that no one could understand the depth of my loss except him. The cavity she left behind merged with the crater of emptiness that he'd created when he left. It made sense to believe he was the only one who could give me solace.

But he hadn't been there, and somehow I'd survived. Or I'd thought I had. Sitting here, speaking of her now, my voice trembles, and I sense the coming wave of grief.

"I knew that," he says softly. "I'm deeply sorry."

The grief halts abruptly, and a storm of rage begins to gather in its place. "You *knew*?"

"I watch out for you. You're always on my radar."

"You knew and yet you let me suffer alone? Couldn't bother to reach out? Send flowers? Or a note?"

"Amelia..." He reaches out to stroke my cheek, but I jerk

my head away. His hand falls to his lap. "You know any contact with you jeopardizes your safety and mine. I couldn't live with myself if you ever became a target in order to hurt me."

I swallow back the rest of my wine in three big gulps then slam the glass down on the table so hard I'm surprised it doesn't break. "*No contact*, but you're here now." Now, when I want him but I don't need him. Now, when it's convenient for him but not when it was urgent for me.

His blue eyes cloud.

"It's complicated. I was already coming to London, and I took precautions when I came here tonight. It's safe. Probably." He shoves a hand through his short hair. "Or maybe not. I don't know." He shakes his head. "It *is* safe. It will be because I won't be here again, and I'm not in the middle of anything at the moment that would draw enemy attention. It was a risky decision, all the same. I'm aware. But, like I said before, I couldn't not see you."

I contemplate him as he works through his justification. Sometimes, when I'm feeling in the mood to pick the scab, I watch James Bond movies. I prefer the idea of a gentleman spy to whatever today's militarized equivalent might be. And I know full well that the girl of the day is always the one in danger, either way.

It's satisfying on some deep, selfish level to realize he's thrown caution to the wind for me. His reality is too foreign, too abstract for me to find truly frightening, so his behavior doesn't feel quite as risky to me as I know it does to him.

It knocks down a barrier between us, and I reach out again to rub the scruff on his jaw while I consider what else to share with him, since he seems keen on talking. There's no one in his own family to inquire after—it was part of what made him the perfect candidate for undercover work. I was only ever his one liability. And I already know he'll share nothing of his actual work.

The frustration of that subsides under the relief that I won't learn anything that will keep me up at night worrying for him.

But that leaves me to bear the brunt of the conversation. It's funny. All the moments, all the individual events that have transpired over the years that I've wanted to share are absent from my mind now. There're too many of them, too many starting places in a large ball of yarn, and I don't know which thread to pick at first to unwind the history of Me Without Him.

So I throw the ball back into his court. "What else do you know, then? Save me the trouble of repeating information you already have on file."

"I know everything on the outside, nothing on the in." He rolls a coil of my dark corkscrew hair between two fingers.

I frown as I try to interpret exactly what he means. Does he simply run a background check from time to time? Or am I under some form of deeper surveillance?

My expression must alert him to my questions, because he clarifies. Slightly. "I know you're a top level manager at Reach, Inc. I was astonished at first when you moved from creative to sales, but, when I thought about it, I realized sales suited you perfectly. I know you put a deposit on this flat with the commission from your first big client. I know the amount in your savings account, that you still haven't taken on driving, and that you spend the little free time you allow your workaholic self at the gym and streaming BBC iPlayer."

He pauses momentarily. "I know that you haven't been lonely."

I'm flabbergasted by this. "*Haven't been lonely?* Where on earth did you possibly get that idea?" I've been *encased* in loneliness. I've been sealed in it like a plum in a bottle of preserves. Loneliness has been the overarching theme of my life for fifteen years, and only worsened by the loss of my grandmother.

"I mean to say your *bed* hasn't been lonely." There's no hint of jealousy or condemnation, and I should be glad because he has no right to either.

But his indifference also smarts, and I pull my hand away so I can wrap my arms around myself.

He picks up on the cue and drops my hair from his grasp, but doesn't sit back. "I came by once. A couple of years ago. Another trip I had to make to London for...business...and I thought, if I could just see you... I didn't mean it, of course, because I knew the minute I did see you, I'd need to talk to you. Then I'd need to touch you."

My gut twists with recognition. I can vividly imagine myself in the same position. One look would never be enough for either of us. Our bodies had always been opposite magnetic poles.

"I couldn't help myself, though. Despite telling myself I wasn't headed here, I ended up in the alley across the street, clinging to the shadows, watching for you to come home."

"What happened?" I ask and hold my breath, as though the story could possibly have a happy ending.

"You came home in a cab. The minute you got out of the car, I lost all ability to breathe. It had been so long since I'd really seen you—pictures and the like are not nearly the same

—and I was completely swept away. I'd forgotten you had that effect on me. It kind of threw me off guard."

"So much off guard that you were able to refrain from coming to my door?" I sound angry, and I am. I had no choice in these matters, and every choice he made that kept him away from me was the wrong choice, as far as I was concerned.

"No, I started toward you. Got as far as putting my foot in the street before I realized you weren't alone." He pauses to let me register that. "The mussed hair seemed your style, but I didn't realize you were into men who wear suits."

"Who said that I was? You automatically assumed it was a romantic situation?"

"You had your hand on his crotch while you put the key in the lock. I didn't have to assume anything."

His smirk increases my rage for reasons I can't explain. I know who the man is instantly from his description. Though I have plenty of fuck-buddies, there's only one who wears a suit that I ever invite back to my house—Dylan Locke. Technically my boss because he owns the company I work for, but he's much more of a friend. A friend who would understand if I cut the night short, no matter the reason, and I would certainly have done that if I'd known Harrington was nearby. There isn't anyone I wouldn't turn away to be with him.

And fuck him for not understanding that.

Fuck him.

My anger is too effervescent inside me. It bubbles up and over, and I can no longer sit and pretend that Harrington hasn't stirred up years' worth of emotional repression. Layer upon layer of all the small hurts that his choices gave me.

I burst from the sofa and grab the dishes on the side table, unsure if I mean to throw them or simply clear them. I turn back toward him, seething. "How dare you? How dare you decide that I wouldn't rather see you? How dare you believe that anyone—anyone!—could fill the hole of loneliness you made inside of me? That there would ever be someone I might love as much as I love you!"

He's practiced at remaining stoic, and he does so now, not letting a single twitch of emotion show on his expression. The blue calm of his eyes, always the same.

Fuck him!

I spin on my heel and deliver the dishes to the kitchen, wanting a reason to put space between us, even though the room is open to the lounge.

"Amelia..." his voice chases after me, soft, gentle. An attempt to calm me.

I slam the plates on the island. "No. You don't get to tell me how to feel about this." When I turn toward him again, I see that he's circled around the sofa, but that's as much as he dares to approach. Good. I don't want to be close enough to smell him, close enough for his presence to again overwhelm me and prevent me from working through this.

"I wasn't trying to hurt you, or make decisions about your life," he says evenly. "I was trying not to interfere."

I practically laugh. "You've interfered more with my life than any other person I've ever known." I don't notice the tears until they're already slipping down my cheeks.

"I shouldn't have told you."

"No, you shouldn't have," I snap, taking an aggressive step in his direction.

He takes a gentler step toward me, putting his hands up

in front of him, either to halt me or show a sign of surrender. "Perhaps I shouldn't have come."

My fury flares. "You shouldn't have *left*!"

And then his restraint breaks, and he's pulling me into his arms. I go willingly, as though I had a choice—which, of course, I don't. I will always be his. I will always go weak in the knees from his presence. I will always end up back in his embrace, suffocating with how much I love him. And I will never work out my feelings with words, because there aren't any for the impossible love between us.

His kiss is frenzied this time, his hands tangled in my hair. I climb his body, wrapping my legs around his waist, clutching at his shirt while my mouth tears frantically at his. His hand lowers to grip my ass, pulling me tighter into him where I can feel his erection pressing against my belly. He spins around and walks us toward the sofa. Once there, he sits me on the back, and pushes up my skirt to reveal the lace pants underneath while I furiously work to undo his jeans. His cock is out and in my hands, even plumper than before, and I pull him closer. I don't want to wait any longer for him, can't possibly wait. I'm edging the gusset of my pants aside with his crown when he reaches toward his back pocket, for his wallet I presume.

"No condom! Please. Please!" I'm begging, desperate for him to comply. There have been too many barriers between us, and I can't bear yet one more.

He hesitates for the slightest fraction of a second. Then he's rocking forward, shoving deep inside me with one solid thrust. And I am complete once again.

"Yes!" I scream, crossing my ankles behind his waist to pull him in further, to keep him from moving away.

Not that he's trying.

He pounds into me at a voracious tempo, as though he can't get deep enough, as though he can't reach as far inside me as he needs to, and isn't that ridiculous because he's already so far inside me, I'm not sure where he ends and I begin. Or if I even begin at all. He might be all that I am anymore. All that I've been since before he left, since he first consumed me over seventeen years ago.

Our mouths remain locked throughout. With his hands on either side of my face, he swallows my moans like they're candy, barely inhaling one before he devours another. It's not the way we typically fucked in the past—Harrington was always the dirtiest of talkers, and with all the men I've been with since, I've yet to meet someone who can top him in this department.

I've longed for those filthy words, dreamed them both asleep and awake, but I'm grateful for this prolonged kiss. Grateful for the connection. Grateful to be reminded just how thoroughly I belong to him. Our kisses say the things we never could.

I'm not usually one for vaginal orgasms, but they aren't completely uncommon, and I feel one building inside me. I unhook my ankles and spread my thighs farther, propping my feet on the back of the sofa on either side of me. It opens me up, and at this angle, his pelvis rubs against my torso and just before he explodes inside me, I detonate with him. I grit my teeth and tremble through the eruption, letting out a low-pitched keening that comes from somewhere so hidden and forgotten, I barely recognize the sound as my own.

Harrington's own release is prolonged, ripping through him at an agonizingly slow rate. It's hypnotic to watch him come apart. It always has been. A man so measured and collected, losing all control in my arms. It makes me heady and drunk on power.

But I'm also exhausted. It feels like this night has been coming for years, feels like I should have been more prepared, but I'm not. The toll is both physical and emotional, and trying to keep up is taking more stamina than I have.

My feet drop off the couch and my legs hang limply at his sides as I gulp in deep breaths in an attempt to recover. Harrington doesn't pull out of me, just presses his forehead against mine and drinks in the same air that I do. I place my palm over the left side of his chest and mentally count his heartbeats as they gradually slow. This heart...it used to belong to me. Does it still?

It's a stupid flicker of doubt. I don't have to ask to know it does, that it always will. The same way mine will always belong to him. No matter the time, no matter the distance.

"I shouldn't have done that," I say when I can speak again. "Shouldn't have told you to go without a condom." It's an easier topic than any other, and that's saying something.

"Are you not on birth control?" He doesn't sound concerned.

"No, I am. And I always use a condom. But I don't know you well enough anymore." God, that hurts to say, and I'm not sure that it's entirely true. I don't want to change the tone of what we just shared with accusations. "I don't know what your sex habits are," I amend.

He pulls back and tilts my chin up so I'm forced to look him in the eyes. "I've only ever gone bare with you."

I knew he wouldn't have remained celibate over all these

years, but this declaration feels very nearly like the same thing. "Why?" I ask, even though I know the answer.

"Because I don't love anyone but you," he says simply.

A sob catches in my throat, and I have to take two deep breaths before I'm able to say anything. "This hurts, you know? It doesn't make anything better. It just hurts."

He sighs. With his hand clapped at my neck, he rubs my jaw with his thumb. "I wasn't going to say anything." He swallows. "That's a lie—I was always going to say this, but I wish that I weren't. I wish that I were strong enough to walk away again, let you live this incredible life you've built for yourself, but I just...I just can't."

My heart trips in my chest. Hope bubbles up from the hidden place it's always hidden. "I don't want you strong enough to walk away again. I don't want you strong enough to crawl. I want you *here*. Is that an option?"

"Not exactly. But the reason I'm in London was because I was offered a promotion. Team leader, of sorts. I haven't accepted it yet, but if I do, I'll no longer be in the field. I'd be in the office, running everything. It means I wouldn't have to be anonymous anymore. I wouldn't be undercover. I could have a life. I could have a life with you."

My pulse races, but I refuse to run with it until I know for sure. "Here? You'd be here?" His long pause lets me know already that it isn't the answer I want.

"I'm afraid not. Mumbai."

India. He's asking me to go with him to India. My throat is tight and my stomach feels heavy. India is another world, one so far removed from my current life that I can't even imagine what ours could look like there.

"It's too much to ask, I know. I shouldn't—"

I cut him off. "Don't take it back. Just, could we maybe discuss it without you inside of me?"

"Of course." He kisses my forehead as he pulls out, as though that might calm the throb of emptiness I feel with him gone. He puts himself away, and takes a step back.

I hop off the sofa and rub the back of my neck as I pace away from him. This is a big thing he's landed me with. An incredible thing, and some free and whimsical part of me wishes it didn't require any consideration, wishes I'd just say yes like I want to and be done with it, but that part of me is small and foreign. I'm not free or whimsical, as a rule. I'm serious and bullheaded. I take risks, but they're practical risks. I'm a tree that's been planted, maybe not where I wanted to be planted, but my roots are deep nonetheless.

I'm not, as much as I wish I was, the same woman he walked away from fifteen years ago.

I circle around the sofa before looking back at him. "Is it safe? You'd said before that any connections you had were liabilities. That they could become targets. Is this different now?"

"It's not as safe as if you were marrying a barrister or a grocer, but, yes, it would be different. A lot of the men and women at this level have spouses. Have families even. It's as close to a nine-to-five position as there is in this business."

"It's a desk job," I say, finally understanding.

"Essentially."

It sounds wonderfully ideal—for me. Not so much for him. "Do you want to accept it? Would you even like a desk job?"

"I would." His tone is uncertain, and he knows it. "I

would for you," he says more sure. "I would love any life with you."

I start to nod my head, because I would love any life with him too. But then I pause because that's not true. I don't want a life with him if he has to give up everything else he loves to get it. That was the whole reason I'd been able to let him walk away the first time—because he loved his job. He loved it as much as he'd loved me.

Years have gone by, but if he still loves me like I know he does, I can't imagine he doesn't still love his job too. And if I am the one to make this choice for him, a piece of him may always long for the love he left behind. Just as it must now, the other way around. It's an impossible choice.

"What happens if you don't accept the job? Do you go back in the field?"

"Yes," he answers simply. Succinctly.

Before I can say anything else, he crosses deliberately to me. "Don't answer now," he says, taking my hands in his. "We have all night together. Let's not think about this at all. I want to be in the moment with you while we have it."

He kisses me, less greedily than before. It's unhurried and thorough. It's passionate, still, and within short minutes, we're on the floor in front of the fireplace. Leisurely, we strip of our clothes, our eyes studying each other with intense interest. I have every centimeter of his landscape memorized, and my fingers and tongue are determined to relearn every inch, mapping the changes since they last explored this land. I take my time, and it's a lengthy survey, almost as long as the expedition his hands take across my own skin.

It feels like hours later when he's stretching over me and pushing inside. We make love slowly, lingering in every stroke, as though we don't have mere hours before morning. As though we have all the time in the world.

I wake before Harry does the next morning. The shadows are still heavy, the first streaks of sunrise not yet on the horizon. I reach for my phone to check the time. My alarm is due to sound in twenty minutes, but I turn it off, knowing that even though I've only slept for a couple of hours, I won't fall back asleep. There's too many jumbled-up thoughts in my head pressing to be sorted. While I was able to brush them aside last night, I can't any longer. There isn't time.

I first try to think about me, about what he's asking me to give up. I don't have a lot of friends, but there are a handful that I'd miss. I'm an only child and my parents are divorced. Could I leave Maman and move to a foreign country without her? Could I give up my job, my *career*—a career I've slaved over, a job that I'm damn good at—for a man I don't really know anymore?

But how can I let him walk away instead?

Instead of finding answers for the future, my mind wanders back to the past. For a long while after he first left, I replayed every detail of our time together on a daily basis. Eventually it became paralyzing. It was too hard to move on when I was stuck in the memory of him, and so I made an intentional effort not to think about it and invest that energy in my career.

It's been a long time since I've retraced these memories, and now that I've opened the dam, they flood over me in a rush.

I'd been just twenty-six when we'd met. It had happened quite by accident, neither of us actually looking for anyone. I'd been wrapped up in advancing my career at the Creative Advertising Agency. After three years on the job, I was still a newbie and the only woman on the sales team, which meant I had to work twice as hard to prove myself. I didn't have the time or energy for anything more than one-night stands and pub flings.

Which was why Harrington was not supposed to last. He was, initially, just a bloke I met at a concert of some no-name band. We'd gone to my place—I still brought men home back then—and had crazy monkey sex all night long. We fell asleep so he stayed the night, and the next morning we woke up to a burst pipe in my building. My entire flat was covered with three inches of water. The tenant manager quickly stepped in to handle the damages, but the cleanup was going to take at least a week, as it had affected several units. There would be no water in the meantime.

Harrington helped me salvage what I could, and, though I'd already said I'd go to a hotel, he offered his flat instead. I couldn't resist his dazzling smile and suave persona. Besides, the sex was incredible, even before we'd memorized each other's preferences. Without hesitation, I agreed.

I was madly in love with him by the end of five days. He seemed to feel the same. We were inseparable after that.

At the time, I knew that Harrington had some government type job that he couldn't talk much about. I knew that he loved it. I knew he was a translator, able to speak Hindi, Punjabi, and Urdu. That was about all I knew. I imagined that he was called in to translate secret messages or help with interrogations. I liked picturing the confident charmer.

My James Bond even then, minus the danger. It was exciting.

We'd been together for eighteen months before he broke down and told me all of it. I'd been pushing for a commitment, a ring. A promise. A possibility for someday, even. When he refused to give it, I was devastated and heartbroken. He hated to hurt me like that. It crushed him. Against all better judgment, against policy and his oath to his officers, he told me he wasn't "just" a translator. He'd been working undercover for the past several years on an important project, and his relationship with me had provided a good cover. He hadn't expected to really fall in love. Now that he was, he was stuck. His obligation was to the job and the people he worked to protect, but his heart belonged to me.

Cold, cold comfort to hear.

"One day," he'd said, "I will be called to a new assignment. I'll be forced to cut off all ties to the people I know. I will not be able to contact you again. I will simply disappear."

It was a tough blow, but one I eventually came to understand. He'd trusted me with his life by telling me what he had, and that was a testimony to his love that I couldn't deny. Over the next several months, he offered me a few more hints to the truth of his situation. They were bitter crumbs from a trail I couldn't follow. He spelled out the rationale for no personal attachments. He explained that his current assignment wasn't qualified as dangerous, but his next assignment would likely not be as safe. The best part was that he was finally able to show me a part of him he'd been hiding, and I quickly learned just how passionate he was for his work. As passionate as he was for me.

Eight months later, just as he'd warned, he was gone.

He made it easy for me, told me to accuse him of cheating. I was to tell our few friends that he'd moved to the United States. *Our* friends were really all *my* friends. No one took his side. No one asked for his forwarding address. No one had a clue there was anything other than the story I gave. They made the appropriate angry noises about me not deserving that, and him not deserving me. No one saw the truth of my pain.

He never asked me to wait for him, and I didn't. Not on purpose. Just, there was never a man who could fill his shoes. Never a man who could fill my soul the way he did. So, although I led an active sex life after he left, I never gave anyone else my heart. But I did give a good portion of it to my career, throwing myself into it with the passion and energy I'd once devoted to Harrington.

Now, my job is what means the most to me. What I am most proud of. It's more than a job, it's my identity. I couldn't imagine walking away from it. It would tear something out of me that could never be replaced. I would do it, though, for Harrington. Even though I barely know the man anymore, I'd do it. But it would damage me.

And there's the impossible choice again, because there is no doubt in my mind that Harry would be just as damaged if he were forced to trade working in the field for a job behind a desk.

"Hey," he says, stirring now beside me. He catches my eye and his sleepy grin fades. "That's the look of a woman who's about to tell me goodbye."

I slide into his arms, and he turns on his side so we're laying face to face. I rub my knuckles across the scruff of his jaw. "I love you too much to go with you," I say quietly. The tears are already stinging my eyes, but I manage to keep them in.

His features darken. I see the emotions wrestling across his face, usually so placid. He's showing me this on purpose, letting down yet another wall. "I asked you to come with me, but I think I love you too much to let you actually do it."

My mouth finds his, and we get lost in long, slow, languid kisses. His fingers drift low and rub my clit, and by the time he rolls me under him, I'm wet and ready for his cock to glide inside me. His thrusts are sweet and unhurried, but each one is purposeful and full of desperate desire and love. Mostly love. So much love.

Later, at the door, it's harder.

"I could quit altogether. I could stay here and be a regular guy."

"You're not a regular guy, Harry."

"I could be."

"This isn't the kind of job a man just walks away from."

"You aren't the kind of woman a man just walks away from."

We kiss again, for a long time. I've given up making it to work on time, but there's a client meeting at ten and a staff meeting at noon, and I'm already being ripped away from the fantasy in front of me by my reality.

Harrington feels the same, I can tell. His eyes say he's already out the door, already half wrapped up in whatever assignment he'll be given next.

And so it's time to say goodbye.

"We aren't over, Amelia," he promises as he steps away. "One day, it will be our time."

"I'm counting on it."

Then I shut the door on my dirty sweet Valentine, take a deep breath, and close my eyes against the tears.

When I open them again, it's just another day without Harrington Steele. But it's also another day closer to when we'll meet again.

Amelia also appears in the Dirty Sweet Duet, Sweet Liar and Sweet Fate .

CHERRY POPPER

This title was originally published in the Laurelin Paige, Kayti McGee sampler. It has been reedited for this edition.

ONE

IF I WERE WRITING an article about tonight, I'd call it *Chase Matthews Discovers Religion.*

Because this right here? This is my idea of goddamned heaven.

When I'd originally agreed to tag along with my buddy Jared to this dinky little bar forty-five minutes outside of our college town, I'd thought we'd have a good time—shoot some pool, flirt with some chicks, use our fake IDs to get a couple beers.

I sure hadn't expected to be crashed against the wall of the back storage room with the legs of the sweetest little blonde in the place wrapped around my waist.

The instant I locked eyes with her, I felt the mutual attraction. There was a pull between us. It had only taken thirty minutes of eye-flirting before she'd made it over to our table. She was alone, which was the universal signal for *I'm into you, and into this, and we don't have to pretend.* At least it had been where I grew up. But I wasn't taking it as a given. In a lot of ways, Colorado wasn't anything like California.

For half a second, when she sashayed over looking that delicious, I worried Jared would try to pick her up instead. I didn't want to have to go alpha on my buddy. But then God intervened—*Chase Matthews Witnesses a Miracle*—and another hot chick scooped Jared off to some dark corner.

And now here I am, with Kira's legs wrapped around my waist and her lips locked on mine.

Man, she tastes good. There was a faint hint of Amaretto Sour, but mostly she tastes of the cherry flavor lip gloss she'd applied and reapplied throughout the evening. Even without the gloss, I suspected she'd taste good. How could she not? Those luscious lips of hers were made to be kissed.

And the things she does with her tongue... Every time she flicks it across the tip of mine, my dick throbs as I imagine it flicking across my crown. And the sexy little sounds she makes in the back of her throat are making my jeans even tighter.

Chase Matthews Verifies the Existence of Angels.

I press her against the wall, relieving some of the weight from my arms so my hand can explore other parts of her body. The new position angles our pelvises more perfectly together. It's both amazing and amazingly uncomfortable all at once.

Trying to ignore the ache in my pants, I distract myself by concentrating on Kira's breasts. If I could just hold one of those perfect little mounds in my palm, I know it will be worth the blue balls I'll have later. I sweep my hand down the side of her torso, then up again, this time a little closer to the object of my desire. Finally, on the third pass, I can't take it anymore. My hand circles around her perky tit and squeezes.

Instead of the protest I'd half expected, she moans. I was nearly exploding already, but that sound has me desperate to make her feel that good again. Within seconds my hand has made its way under her T-shirt and slipped under the cup of her bra. Had I thought I'd made it to heaven before? Well, I was wrong. Because *this* was definitely heaven. Soaring on the wind, floating on air, heaven.

Then she says the magic words—the words every guy wants to hear when his dick is painfully hard and his hand is wrapped around her breast—"I have a condom."

Sweet Jesus, I'm going to get laid in the back of this dive bar.

But I'm not an asshole. I know the rules of chivalry. I break from her lips and kiss up to her ear, delighting at the shiver that rolls through her body when I nip at her lobe. "Are you sure?"

"Yeah. I'm sure."

Score!

I feel instantly harder, if that's even possible. If the whole event was only about me, I'd have the condom on and be inside her before she could blink. And since I'll likely never see Kira again, I could easily get away with selfish sex.

But I won't let it ever be said that Chase Matthews took a girl for granted. Ever. Setting her down so I have both my hands free, I slip my fingers up her skirt and under the elastic ribbing at the leg of her panties. My thumb slides between her folds until I find the hood of her clit. With alternating featherlight swirls and concentrated pressure, I treat her as good as I know how.

Boosting my confidence further, Kira sighs deeply at my touch. "Yes," she mumbles. "Oh God, yes."

Her features hypnotize me—the way her mouth parts, the way she peers up at me from hooded lids—it's beautiful in a way I've never noticed. Do all women look this gorgeous when they're mid-clit rub? Maybe I just never paid attention. Maybe I had been taking them for granted.

When I feel her body start to tighten, I move my fingers further down. Damn, she's already so wet. So ready for me. I'll have to make this good, because I have a feeling I'm not going to last long inside her.

I glide two fingers in, my thumb still circling above.

Immediately, she cries out.

I reclaim her mouth, swallowing her sounds before she alerts the staff that we've taken over their storage room. *Shit.* The noises she makes when she comes are even more beautiful than her face. She is a revelation.

At this point I am turned on like a megawatt light bulb and I can't bear the thought of waiting any longer to be inside her. Time to suit up.

"Should I get the condom?" Kira asks against my lips.

Apparently she's on the same wavelength.

"Actually, I have one." Thank God, too, because I hate the idea of breaking apart for her to rummage through her purse. Even letting her go to dig in my pocket is almost more than I can take. I retrieve the square foil from my wallet then push my pants and briefs down just enough for my dick to spring free.

Ah, much better.

Kira removes her panties while I rip open the condom and poise it over my cock. When I glance up, I notice her eyes glued to my shaft. Damn, that's hot too. Is there anything this chick does that isn't hot?

"Do you want to put it on?" I ask. Maybe she's one of those girls who prefer to participate in this part. Or maybe I just want to feel her hands on me.

"No, thank you. But I'd like to watch, if you don't mind."

Mind? No, I definitely don't mind.

I take my time rolling it on, basking in the heat of her watchful eyes. Calming down so that I can last longer. When I finish, I reach for her again, but she puts her palm up to stop me.

"Wow. That's big." Her brown eyes are wide. "I mean, not in a bad way or like I'm worried about it fitting or... God, I sound like a moron."

I can't help grinning. "Big is totally an acceptable description." It's true, too. Something I've always been proud of. I hold an arm out to her. "Now, come here."

Instantly she's on me, her mouth locked with mine, leg wrapped around my hip. I bunch her skirt up around her waist and position myself at her entrance. Then I'm sliding in and *Chase Matthews Has Died and Gone to Heaven.* Jesus, she feels good. Way good. Tight and wet and fucking awesome.

"Oh, wow."

Did she just read my mind?

"Wow." She says it over and over, seemingly surprised. I try not to let that offend me. "Wow. Oh, wow!" Her words trail away into incomprehensible gibberish.

Then talking is over. Hell, thinking is over. I kiss along her jaw and neck as I move in and out of her. The sexy noises she made earlier are nothing in comparison to the angelic sounds she makes now. They accompany each thrust, echoing in my head like a carnal symphony. I wish I could make it last forever—the feel of her, the sight of her, the music of her.

But, of course, I can't. Too soon I can feel it starting, and then I'm coming, driving into her with a last long stroke. I groan her name into her ear as I do—which is weird. Normally I never call out anything but God and Jesus when I'm climaxing.

Perhaps it's a good thing, then, that I'll never see her again. That this tryst with Kira is a fuck in the stockroom and nothing more. Because otherwise—and I don't want to sound all girly about it—otherwise I just might fall in love.

TWO

AN ENTIRE SEMESTER LATER, I'm still thinking about her. Kira. Kira Larson, according to what her girlfriend yelled as we emerged from the back room, slightly mussed and glowing all over. I stare at the blank document on my computer screen, the blinking cursor hypnotizing me. This isn't really the way I want to spend such a beautiful February afternoon, but my brain just isn't working right.

It's not like I haven't met any other girls in my first few months on campus. Hell, I've met lots of girls. Girls who'd seemed interested, even. But every time I think of asking someone out or hooking up with a chick from my swipe app, all I can see is chocolate brown eyes and hear the sexy little sounds of that angel.

Fuck, I'm basically pussy-whipped. By a girl I met *once* in a town forty-five minutes away. Time to move on. Past time, really. Maybe I need to rip off the Band-Aid. Go out tonight and find someone to replace her memory. Yeah, that's what

I'll do. Just as soon as I get this stupid paper finished. Which at this rate, will be some time next week.

Jared knocks as he sticks his head through my open door. "Hey, you coming with me?"

I've known Jared for ages. We hadn't been best buds or anything, but we'd been friendly enough. Same crowd at school, same baseball letter jackets. So when he found out I was looking for a good school to follow up on my community college Associate's Degree, Jared had suggested I check out University of Northern Colorado. The tuition is good and the school has a strong Education Department. It seemed like a good place for me to pursue my teaching degree.

Now I live with Jared, a spur-of-the-moment decision, in a house we share with six other guys. Most of them are a little more aggressively jock than I like, but we all get along well enough. They're respectful, if not the neatest of roommates.

I lean back in my swivel chair and stretch until my back pops. Maybe I ought to take a break from staring at this screen. Grab a coffee or something. "Depends. Where you heading?"

Jared leans against the doorframe and gives me a wicked grin. "The Cherry Savers rally. They're the ones that are publicly saving themselves for marriage."

I raise a brow, obviously missing something. "Why the hell would we want to go there?"

"Those chicks won't bang, but they give the best head on campus. It is known."

I hide my eye roll by refocusing on my laptop. "You're a total dog."

"And you aren't? At least I got a number last time I hooked up in a bar."

"Touché." And why hadn't I at least asked for Kira's number? I've been kicking myself about it ever since. But when we'd parted it had been so simple and easy and perfect —I hadn't wanted to mess it all up by asking to see her again and being turned down. A girl like that wouldn't want to date the guy she hooked up with in a bar. She would want the guy she could bring home to her parents with a nice story about meeting in a grocery store, or at a football game.

No, I'm good without that embarrassing memory tarnishing the one of the sex. This situation is fine. And there is no way in hell I would be caught going to a virginity club meeting. *Chase Matthews Falls From Grace.* "I think I'll just stay in. I need to figure out what I'm doing for this article due Monday. But thanks for the invite."

Jared shrugs and bends to tie his shoes. "Suit yourself."

I thunk my head down on my desk and sigh. This article is killing me. Now that I'm all settled in here, I'd decided to pick up an extracurricular. I'd had a regular column on the paper at my last school and figured I was a shoo-in for at least an occasional feature in UNC's campus journal. Turns out the editor is a dick. Or just unreasonable. He'd taken no more than a three second glance at the copies of my portfolio before shoving it back across the desk.

"Eight hundred words," the editor had said. "Something about UNC campus life. Due Monday. Then I'll decide."

Jesus, really? "Excuse me, but I'm not familiar enough with student life yet to be able to find something in such a short time," I told him. "I spent most of my first semester studying." Given a week, I could pull together something totally brilliant. A weekend? Not likely.

"You could do a Valentine's piece if you prefer."

That was a hard no.

The editor had tilted his head and narrowed his eyes. "Then what use are you to me? Journalists aren't supposed to be *familiar* with their stories. That's what bloggers are for."

So now I have two choices: abandon the idea of working on the paper or pull something out of my ass. I spent all Friday night researching the school website, looking for anything that might trigger an idea. I ended up with a whole bunch of nothing. Reading about student life wasn't going to do anything but bore me to death. I need to actually experience campus life here—outside of the bars.

Wait a sec...my head shoots up with the force of a sudden idea. "Hey, Jared. Is this rally a big thing? Like, is it newsworthy?"

Jared wiggles his brows. "You could totally write an article on it if that's what you're thinking."

"Let me get my notebook."

TWENTY MINUTES LATER, we're enjoying the unseasonal warmth at the field by Gunter Hall, standing around the band shell with a crowd of nearly two hundred people waiting for the rally to begin. A group of women are circled on the short stage and a guy keeps tapping on the microphone —testing it or just being annoying, I honestly can't even tell.

I scan my surroundings. "Are all these people virgins?" There is no *way* there are this many prudes on campus. Is there?

"Hardly," Jared says. "Lots of people are just here for the

spectacle. The Cherry Savers are the ones wearing the T-shirts."

I hadn't noticed the abundance of black tees beneath the jackets in the crowd until now. The majority of wearers are female, but I spot a few guys wearing them too. I truly don't understand. Why anyone—particularly a dude—would be so blatantly proud of their choice to remain "pure" is so foreign to me. Especially when their pride involves wearing that awful shirt. They have a picture of a cherry bunch ala Ms. Pac Man and the words *Life's Full of Pits, Save a Cherry*. I don't even want to figure out what that's supposed to imply.

Like, is having sex supposed to be the pits? And if you refrain, then you miss out on life's pits? Because intercourse is the root of all the world's problems?

Okay, I *am* trying to figure it out, just not with any satisfying success.

Jared leans in close so only I can hear him. "Most of the other guys here are stalking prey like us."

Like you, I correct in my mind. *Chase Matthews Is Above This*. I set my phone to camera mode and prop my notebook under my arm while I snap a few pictures of the crowd.

"That girl over there." Jared nods at a brunette wearing the club's uniform. "That's Wanda Low. Guess what her nickname is?"

I cringe as I make the most obvious guess. "Wanna Blow? Original, Jared."

"It so totally fits her, though," Jared says, laughing at the ridiculous joke. "I'll hook you up. All you gotta do is say the word."

"Maybe next time." There would be no next time. I was

uncomfortable with the whole scenario. Someone ought to warn these girls.

I pocket my phone and pull the pen from the spiral of my notebook to jot down a few notes:

Mostly women

Seventy-two members according to the T-shirt count

Religious based?

Stupid-ass slogan

The whole thing is certainly weird, but that isn't really the best approach to take on a journalism piece. The assignment wasn't gonzo, it was objective. I'll have to gather some more info before I can determine my angle.

A girl's voice comes over the speakers, drawing my attention to the stage. The girl is pretty enough. That isn't the reason she's a virgin. I add that to my notes:

Not ugly girls

Then I think twice and cross it out. I'm supposed to be a better man than Jared, but just five minutes around these bros has me group-thinking with them. I shake my head.

"Thank you so much for coming out today," the girl says. "I'm excited to see all this support for this wonderful group we've formed. As most of you already know, I'm Shalinda Wild—" She pauses to let the small applause (mostly male) die down. "And while I've thoroughly enjoyed my time as Princess Cherry Saver, my run is over. And now I have to pass the chastity belt on to my successor."

Chastity belt. How cute. I write the terms in my notebook, making sure I have them all down accurately for my piece.

Jared leans in again to whisper, "Hey, do you think that means she'll spread 'em now?"

I open my mouth to tell Jared to shut his trap, or maybe just to punch him, but freeze before I can get a sound out. That girl—the one walking up to the podium, the one taking the key from the Princess Cherry Saver as she begins her reign—I *know* that girl. And I don't really know any girls in Colorado.

Except one.

"Holy shit, Chase! Is that who I think it is?"

The pen suddenly feels sweaty in my grip. "Yeah, I think so."

Man, all semester I've been dying to see her again, and this? This is how? Leading a rally for virginity? Well, if this doesn't put a thousand questions in my mind. And on top of the confusing nature of the situation, I'm turned on just at the sight of her thick dark-blonde hair and dimpled cheek. She looks different like this—from afar, unaware that I'm gazing at her. God, she is just as beautiful as I remember. It makes me feel all funny in my chest, like it's hard to catch a breath, like no matter how deeply I expand my lungs, the air that moves through them isn't enough.

"That's not really her, is it?" Jared claps a hand on my back, and finally I can breathe again.

"No, it's her all right." *Kira Larson.* I feel a mixture of relief and trepidation as she begins her speech about all the benefits of waiting until marriage. On the one hand, she herself isn't a virgin. That's a betrayal somehow—either to me or to the crowd gathered around.

On the other hand, *there she is.* Standing in front of me. Looking gorgeous.

"Goddammit, man, you lied to me!" Even Jared seems to

get the sense of betrayal. "There's no way the President of Cherry Savers let you put your dick in her."

And that was the confusion of the matter. Why *had* she let me bang her? It had been her idea, even. I'd been careful not to pressure her. The question left me irritated. "They're called Princesses, Jared."

"What-the-fuck-ever they're called, you did not get American in that pie."

"And if you did get American in it," Jared lowers his voice, "that story has to be told."

A story that had to be told. That's what good reporting is, isn't it? "What do you mean? Like an exposé?"

Jared shrugs. "Well, yeah. Because that's some serious hypocrisy. Why would she even do that? What's the point? Maybe she's a pathological liar."

And isn't that the sixty-four-million-dollar question? "I have no idea why. But I'd be interested in her reasoning." *Very interested.*

"You and the entire house." Jared's expression says he's already imagining the guys' reactions. Imagining and enjoying. "I can't wait to tell Marcus. He's been trying to pick a Cherry Saver since freshman year."

"No. Don't do that." I have to think about this. *Princess Cherry Saver Is No Saint.* It would make for a great article.

Except, she probably has her reasons for the dual life. I don't know the first thing about her. Do I really want to betray her trust like that?

Although she sure betrayed mine.

Whatever. I *don't* know her. This is a chance to prove my cutthroat journalist skills. "Don't tell anyone, Jared. Not yet. The other idea was better."

Jared's brow wrinkles with confusion. "An exposé? What, you going to write your article about popping the Queen Cherry Saver's cherry?"

"Oh, her cherry was already popped." *Wasn't it?* Yeah, it had to be.

"All right then, an article exposing Queenie's popped cherry?"

"It's Princess." I take a deep breath, square my shoulders, and swallow the last bit of hesitation telling me not to write this story. "And yeah, why not?"

Jared breaks into a grin. "Exactly. Why the hell not?"

THREE

JARED LEAVES me alone as soon as the rally is finished. He's likely making his move—or, attack, rather—on one or more of the several Cherry Savers he had singled out as potential hookups. He didn't exactly say, and I wasn't exactly sure I wanted to know.

As for me, I stay back from the stage and keep my eyes on Kira as the scene moves into cleanup mode. She has a small crowd surrounding her but to get the information I need, I have to get her alone. At least, that's the reason I tell myself that I want her alone. Not because I still have any desire to nip along her jawline or wrap my fingers in her hair. It's all about the story. Yeah, that's what it is.

My mind replays the things she'd said during her event speech, how she'd been so sincere in her delivery. "Sex should not define our relationships with the people we want to spend our entire lives with," she had said. "How can we separate lust from love when we allow hormones to be in control?

"And when we finally find the person—that special person that we want to dedicate ourselves to—what better gift is there to give him or her than our body, untouched and undefiled? What a way to say, 'You're the most important person in my world. I waited *for you.*'"

That last sentiment had gotten Kira a cheer from her audience.

I, on the other hand, still don't know how to react. Obviously Kira didn't really believe the things she said. But what parts of it were true, which were just rhetoric? Was our brief affair simply a case of hormones out of control? Or did it make me special—someone worthy of her "gift"?

Of course it's the former. I shouldn't even let myself think about the other option. We had sex in a stockroom, for crying out loud. It was completely hormone-incited. For some reason, admitting that to myself makes me feel bitter.

It also strengthens my resolve to get this story, to "out" the girl who is messing with my head without even trying.

Soon, the microphone and speakers are down and the crowd is dispersing. Kira shouts after the group she's been chatting with, "I'll meet you over there."

Then, finally, she's alone. I watch her gather her belongings into her shoulder bag. This is my chance to get the answers I need. I walk up to the stage, catching her as she steps off the bottom step. "Kira?"

"Yeah?" She turns toward me, her eyes so bright and her smile so pure, my knees nearly buckle from the force.

Then she recognizes me. I see the moment it happens, too —her expression falls, her face loses its color. "Oh. It's you."

She looks so horrified at the sight of me that I almost feel bad. *Almost.* Then I'm just pissed. I can't have imagined the spark between us at the bar. She owes me more than a blanched look and an *oh.* "Yep. It's me. Chase. Chase Matthews."

Kira scans the area around us. Apparently satisfied we're alone, she visibly relaxes. She lowers her eyes, a blush touching her cheeks. "I remember your name." Her voice is soft, flirty, even.

"You do?" I hadn't really thought she wouldn't recall who I am. Just, all of a sudden, I'm not entirely sure what to say.

"Of course I do. Why wouldn't I?" She pushes a strand of her hair behind her ear and for half a second I wish it were me touching her hair, touching her ear, kissing her. Sliding my thumbs over her pert nipples, following them with my tongue.

The Temptation of Chase Matthews.

I force my gaze away and shrug. I have to focus on the story. "I don't know. No reason."

God, I have to get a hold of myself. Picturing her naked is not helpful. This is not going to get me the article I want, the article I *need.* The relief from thinking about her day in and day out. I take a step toward her and lean my arm against the proscenium of the shell. I stare at her, breathing evenly, until I feel better. More in control.

"I guess I'm just surprised to see you again. Especially under these circumstances." I gesture around.

"You're surprised to find I'm a Cherry Saver, you mean."

"Well, yes." I had been prepared for a lot of answers, but not pure bluntness. So much for being the one in control.

But if she can be straightforward, so can I. "Because I'm pretty sure you didn't actually save your cherry."

"I suppose you would be pretty sure of that, wouldn't you?"

Her cheeks grow pinker and it's a jolt straight to my groin. God, she looks gorgeous like this—all flushed and innocent. Even wearing that stupid-ass T-shirt under her North Face. "Yes. Very sure." For another long moment I'm taken back to that night, to her legs wrapped around my waist, to those sweet, sweet sounds that still vibrate in my ears.

Dammit, how does she screw with my focus so easily?

I run a hand over my face. "Which is why I'm confused. I'm sure you can understand."

"I can."

But that's all she offers. No explanation, just those two words. This is going to be tougher than I hoped. "So why, then? Why did you get up there and play Princess Cherry Saver when you don't believe any of that crap?"

She moves around me to the back of the band shell, gesturing for me to follow.

Good. Now we're in a more private location.

Wait—*is* that good? Because now the flashbacks of the last time we were alone are even more prominent in my mind.

Kira obviously doesn't have the same thoughts on hers. Her brow furrows in irritation. "Who says I don't believe that crap?"

"You're kidding me, right?" Is this all a setup by Jared? Maybe I'm on some sort of prank show. Only there aren't any cameras that I can see.

Kira adjusts her bag on her shoulder. "There are some really good principles in the Cherry Saver Manual."

"There's a manual?" What other principles could there be besides *keep your legs shut*?

Never mind. I don't want to know. "Don't answer that. Whatever the principles, you obviously don't follow them."

"Who says?"

"I had sex with you the first time I met you!" That *had* happened, hadn't it? Because it's starting to feel like maybe it had all been a dream. A very good dream, but unreal nonetheless.

Kira looks down at her boot as she kicks at a patch of grass. "Yeah, well, anyone can make a mistake."

That zing hit like a knife to my chest. "You're calling me a mistake?" Hopefully she hadn't noticed the slight quiver in my voice as I said that. I already feel completely whipped where she's concerned.

"Not you, exactly. I'm calling sex a mistake." She sighs. "I should have waited."

"Like, until we'd been on a date or something?" It *was* kinda slutty how we'd jumped each other in a bar. Also really fucking hot.

Or does she mean something else? "Until we were married?"

She shakes her head, not meeting my eyes. "Just in general. I should have waited in general."

I take in her words, finally understanding her meaning. *No, no, no.* That's impossible. It can't be, but... "Are you trying to tell me you were a virgin?"

"Shh, keep it down, will you?" She grabs my arm, pulling

me even further behind the band shell. "Of course I was a virgin."

"No way." I try to ignore the tingling of my skin where she touched me and concentrate on the facts of our tryst. "You had a condom."

Her cheeks grow rosy again. "What can I say? I was raised to be prepared."

"There is no way you hadn't had sex before." I don't know if I want to believe it.

"Are you calling me a liar?"

I raise a brow. "Um, considering the speech you just gave to that crowd, yeah, I am."

"Well, I'm not lying about this."

I think back to the way Kira had stared at my dick. She *had* seemed a little bewildered at the sight. Was it because she'd never seen one live and in person?

Nah, that couldn't be it. And there were other things, other signs I can't ignore. "But you knew what you were doing." Like how she'd squeezed around me, the way she'd bucked her hips to feed me deeper into her.

She thrusts out her jaw defiantly. "It's not like I haven't done my research."

"What the hell are you talking about?"

"I read books, Chase. I've seen...videos."

The thought of Kira watching porn is overwhelmingly awesome, and I can't even respond.

"Forget it." She blows out a breath of frustrated air. "Point is—some things are natural. You know?"

"No, I don't know." My first time had been super awkward and over in a rush. Nothing like what I experienced with Kira. "First time sex is *not* like that normally."

"How so?"

"It's usually pretty bad."

She peers up at me, her brown eyes sparkling. "Really? So I wasn't bad?"

"No. There was nothing bad about you and me at all." I hold her gaze for several seconds, drowning in the depth of her chocolate pools. Something stirs inside me. From the burn of it, I'd say it's just being horny, but this is a little higher, in my chest. Nearer to my heart.

Whoa. This is so not happening.

I run a hand through my hair. She couldn't have been a virgin. Could. Not. Not because it isn't a possibility, given what she's just told me, but because I don't want it to be true. Because that would make me the worst kind of asshole—taking her virginity in the back of a bar. So it can't be true. "Isn't there supposed to be blood or something? You know, your first time?"

"Sometimes."

"And other times?"

She rolls her eyes. "Let's just say that if thirteen years of horseback riding didn't break my hymen then I'm pretty sure that the excessive masturbation did."

"Okay, wait." I put a hand up to pause her. "Excessive masturbation?" If I didn't before, I definitely have a semi now.

Kira throws her hands up. "That's not the point! The point is, I *was* a virgin, okay? No man before you had ever entered the Garden of Eden."

I have to adjust my notebook over my groin. "All right, all right." And maybe that *does* explain all her "wow"-ing the night of the deed—it was a totally new sensation. Fuck, yeah, that *would* be surprising. I feel a little bad. "Sorry for assuming."

"Thank you." She leans against the band shell, dropping her bag to the ground.

She could still be lying, of course. She has valid reasons for keeping up the pretense.

But something about the look in her eyes tells me she's sincere. As much as I don't want to believe it, I do.

And there's something hot about *that* too.

I take a step toward her, strategically readjusting the notebook, and lean one shoulder against the wall. "So, really? I was your first?"

She glances up at me, then nods her head, a slight smile on her lips.

Great. Now I sound like the asshole I was afraid this would make me, getting my kicks off of being the one who popped her. That would make me just as bad as Jared. It's all coming out wrong, so I start over. "I just wish I would have known," I tell her softly.

"Why, so you could snag my panties as a memento?" Sassy.

"Come on, I'm not a total dick." I lean in, and I swear she does the same. We're so close. Thoughts of my article are no longer my priority. Sure, I still need to write it, but now, at this very moment, all I want to do is explore this connection. I wanted to be honest with this girl who had—to use her words —given me her "gift."

"I would have done things differently." I reach out to finger a loose strand of her hair, my fingers brushing her cheek as I do. "Gone slower. Made it special somehow."

She turns her head, locking eyes with me. "I thought it was special just the way it was."

"You did?" That burning in my chest intensifies.

"Yeah, I did."

Then all I can do is kiss her, kiss her the way I should have kissed her the first time—slowly, sweetly. She responds perfectly, molding her mouth to mine, sighing softly.

I drop my notebook, put a hand on her cheek and turn into her, taking my time before I slide my tongue between her lips, taking my time yet again before I plunge further into the recesses of her mouth. It's like reciting poetry, the way she tastes. Like honey-dripped words that dance on my lips before sinking deeper into my soul.

This is how she deserves to be kissed. Sure, my dick is rock-hard and pressing tightly against my jeans, but I can ignore that. For her. Without knowing her that well, the way I suddenly want to, I do know this one thing—Kira Larson is the real deal.

It surprises me, this revelation. It's not at all where I thought this day was going to go, nor the confrontation itself. But it isn't unwelcome.

When I finally break away, we're both breathless. She offers an adorable smile, her lips shining and swollen.

I take a step back from her—both physically and mentally —and look her over. On one hand, I still have a story to write and I shouldn't let a simple kiss get in the way of a spot on the paper.

On the other, how could I let her walk away? Not again. I need to spend more time with her. I need to know what all of this means. "Look, are you doing anything later? Or now?"

I can't say for sure if my motivation for asking is to learn more for the article or because I suddenly can't stand to be away from her. I tell myself I don't have to decide yet. I can wait and see how the day plays out.

Kira twists a piece of her hair around her finger. "Not really. I'm supposed to meet my friends at The Kitchen, but I can blow them off. Are you inviting me back to your apartment?"

I nearly choke on my own saliva. "Wow, I wasn't. But now I want to." *Really* want to. But haven't I just decided she's better than that? That she deserves more? Regardless of what happens with my journalism career, I'm going to take Kira on a proper first date. "I was going to ask if you'd like to grab some coffee."

Her eyes light up though she tries to hide it. "Coffee could be good. Yeah, let's do coffee."

"And my apartment?" Okay, so I'm still a guy. And my dick is throbbing.

She bites her lip as if considering. "Why don't we play it by ear?"

"I think I can live with that."

FOUR

"THE BLUE MUG OKAY?" I ask, playing it cool after retrieving my notebook from the ground.

"Duh. Where else would we go?"

Honestly I wasn't sure. I've been told The Blue Mug at Margie's was the best in town, but frankly, it's also the only coffee shop I've gone to so far. I'm a creature of habit. Plus, it's close by, only a block away from where we are.

Together we head across the grass, passing a group of guys playing Frisbee golf outside Frasier Hall. I step a little closer to Kira. I'm not sure if I want people to know she's with me so I'll look cooler or so they won't think she's available. Admittedly, either reason is completely immature. I can't help it. She makes my inner caveman come out.

And is it my imagination, or did Kira also just step closer to me when one of the Frisbee guys smiles at her? Maybe we're both being immature. It's a nice thought, anyway.

We're so close now that I could reach out and grab her

hand if I wanted to. And I do want to. Electric currents are streaming from my fingers to hers, like a magnet pulling me toward her. So close...

But I can't. Stupid, since I've already had my dick inside her. But it just feels too intimate to hold her hand right now, to admit to the both of us that I wanted to take this public.

God, I'm a real chickenshit. And I've been so in my head over what this looks like, we're already halfway to our destination and we still haven't said a word to each other.

Surely I can manage conversation. I clear my throat. "So tell me something about yourself."

She glances at me. "Like what?"

"Anything."

"Why?"

I shrug. "To get to know each other. That's what people do on dates. "

Her brows shoot up. "This is a date?"

Oh, shit. Maybe I *can't* manage conversation. "Oh—I don't—I guess it doesn't have to be." I can feel my cheeks warming. I had just assumed... This is so embarrassing.

Chase Matthews Puts Foot in Mouth.

Kira breaks into a smile. "Geez, I'm just kidding. Chill out." She lowers her eyes. "Actually, I didn't know if it was a date or not." She peeks up at me from under her fantastically long lashes and all my masculine pride returns.

It's kind of awesome to realize she's as tentative about this as I am. That neither of us is on sure footing. "Well, if I say it's a date, would you still be here?"

"I would."

Hallelujah! "Then it's totally a date. No questions asked."

She laughs. Do girls' laughs always sound so soft and

sweet? Suddenly it feels like I've never really listened to one before. Hearing Kira laugh is like hearing laughter for the first time.

My hand brushes hers, and I decide to err on the side of boldness. "Since it's a date, I can hold your hand, right? People do that on first dates, don't they?"

"While they get to know each other? Yeah, I think they do."

"Awesome." I slip my hand into hers and marvel at how perfectly they seem to fit, as though they had been waiting for each other. Two puzzle pieces. Perhaps it has something to do with how intimate we've already been. That has to be it. It has nothing to do with being "made for each other" or "fated."

That sort of thinking is just ridiculous.

Especially when I have an article to write. I have to keep my eye on the prize. Even if I'm feeling more and more dread at the prospect with every step we take. "So then. Something about yourself."

"Oh, yes." She twists her lip while she ponders and damn, I can't take my eyes off the sexy gesture. "Are we going deep or staying superficial?"

It seems to me we've already gone pretty deep.

I bite back saying it out loud just in time. I'm not going to talk to her like she's one of my roommates.

"Maybe we could start light and then delve...further in." I cringe even as it's still coming out of my mouth. I was specifically avoiding the word *deep*, but that was somehow even weirder-sounding. Luckily, she doesn't blink. Maybe she didn't notice.

"Sounds good. Nothing's ever really superficial anyway.

Okay, easy one—I'm a sophomore and I just declared my major."

"Which is?"

"Speech pathology."

"Nice." Really, I know nothing about speech pathology. I rack my mind to come up with a suitable comment without sounding like a moron. So much for my stellar conversation skills. "UNC has a good program for that, don't they?"

"Yep. Nationally renowned." She seems impressed that I know that. The only reason I do, of course, is because of the time I spent scanning the school's website earlier, trying to come up with an article topic. "Your turn."

"I just transferred in as a junior. I got my Associate's Degree last spring in English at SDCC."

"SDCC?"

I keep forgetting I'm in a place where the acronym isn't familiar. "San Diego City College. Now I'm going for an education degree."

She nods, her hair catching the light as it bounces on her shoulder. "UNC's also known for their education program."

"That's why I'm here." And at the moment, I couldn't be happier about it.

Reluctantly, I let go of Kira's hand to hold the door open for her at The Blue Mug. Inside was less crowded than it had been on the last weeknight that I'd come. Then, study groups had dominated the scene and it was hard to find an empty table. Now, there are still a few books cracked open, but there are several places to sit.

After we order steaming hot drinks and a couple items from the bakery, we settle in at a table on the patio to enjoy both the privacy and the sunshine.

This time it's easy to pick the conversation back up. "Do you like it here?" I ask. As a transplant, I'm always curious about other people's experiences.

"At The Blue Mug or UNC?"

I shrug. She can tell me anything she wants in that musical voice of hers. "Either."

"I love The Blue Mug. Best place ever. Especially on Open Mic Night."

My mind wanders momentarily as I imagine going to an Open Mic Night with Kira. We'd hold hands across the table, sharing a plate of scones like we are now. Maybe I'd even get up and recite some poetry for her. Not an original, that would be too private, but she'd probably love Neruda...

I catch myself mid-fantasy. What the fuck is this about? I barely know the woman. Sure, I'm enamored with her gaze and her laugh and the way her tits look under that shirt, but I'm also very seriously considering ruining her life. So why am I creating some make-believe future for us? I have to cut it out.

Don't I?

If I'm serious about this article, then yeah, I definitely do. I slide my finger absentmindedly down the spiral of my notebook, letting the metal remind me why I came.

"What's with the notebook?"

I freeze, feeling like a kid caught with my hand in the cookie jar. It's silly, too, since I haven't even written anything about Kira yet. Just *planning* to.

And it's that feeling, the mixture of guilt and shame, that make up my mind for me.

I've been going back and forth in my mind for the last hour about this exposé, which right there should be telling me it's a bad idea. I'm so into her right now. The thought of writing about her is one thing, but the idea of her seeing it—of how she would then see *me*—no.

I'll write a recap of the Cherry Savers rally like I originally intended. It can be wry, it can be snarky, but it can't out her. And if it isn't enough to get me on the paper, then fuck it. I'd rather miss out on being a reporter than miss out on her.

A weight I didn't realize I was carrying lifts as I make my choice.

"It's nothing," I tell her, tossing the notebook to the chair next to me. "I had this dumb idea that I was going to get an assignment done today."

Her brows crease. "Do you need to work on it?"

"Nah." I don't want to say much about it, still feeling guilty at what I had nearly talked myself into doing, but at the same time I do want to tell her about myself. Especially when she's looking up at me with such interest in her expression. Like I'm as fascinating as I like to think I am in my best articles.

"I was thinking about trying out for the school paper and the editor needs an audition article. So I was messing around with some ideas. I didn't get anywhere though."

"Do you want me to help you brainstorm?"

It's adorable the way she focuses this concern on me. Exactly the opposite of how I'd focused on her. *Chase Matthews Is a Super-Douche.* "No way. Homework on a Saturday? I'd much rather take in the sights with you."

"That's a laugh." Kira nibbles on the corner of a scone. "Besides this place, there is not a single sight in this town worth seeing."

I meet her eyes as she licks honey off her thumb. She's so

beautiful to look at—sensual and intriguing and just plain cute. I could stare at her for hours, I'm sure of it. "I don't know. I'm looking at one right now."

"What?" She flushes when she gets it, and I'm charmed.

But I play it cool and change the subject. "I was just wondering—"

She cuts me off. "Why am I part of Cherry Savers?"

Again with getting straight to the point. That actually *is* the question I want to ask most. But even more than that, I want to get to know more about Kira Larson. And if I move too quickly to the Cherry Savers subject, she'll think that's all I care about. And even though I'm still wildly curious, and prepared to spend hours discussing that perfect pussy, I'll start out slowly.

"Actually, I was wondering how you ended up here. You don't seem to be particularly fond of the town. Is it because of the speech program?"

"Not really. It was sort of a given I'd go to UNC. I'm from here."

"From Greeley?" That surprises me. I hadn't met anyone in my classes actually from the town yet and just assumed most of the students came from elsewhere. Apparently not.

"Born and raised."

I lean into the table and lower my voice. "Do you ever get used to the smell?" Besides being a college town, Greeley is a ranching community and the smell of slaughter always seems to lay in the air. On warm nights especially, the breeze heightens the stench. It's a far cry from the salty ocean air I'm used to.

Kira laughs. "I suppose you do get used to it. I rarely notice it until someone points it out."

"Then there's hope I might survive this place yet."

"I didn't say that."

Damn, I want to kiss that cute little smile of hers away. But I'm trying to move slow. Which I am fully aware is a contradiction since we've already banged. Whatever. This is how I get to know what's inside the straight-shooting little angel in front of me.

"Then why did you stay? You could go elsewhere. Or are you a Momma's girl?"

"Shut up." She punches my shoulder. And, despite the fact that she has a fairly good right hook, I might tease her again just to feel more of her touch. "I couldn't pass up the tuition. My father's on the staff. It gives me a pretty hefty discount."

"Daddy's girl, then."

"Please. No."

I'm a tad disappointed when she doesn't slug me again.

She takes a swallow of her latte. "Trust me. I'd rather be somewhere where I'm not under his eye all the time. I could be more myself. Or figure out who that is, exactly. You know?"

"Are you taking classes in his department or something? Because you could always just transfer."

She sighs. "Kinda hard when the entire school is his department." Kira scrunches up her little nose as if hesitant to go on. "He's the school president."

"Oh, fuck!" *Dammit, that was crass.* "I mean, shit." *Is that even any better?* "I mean..." I take a deep breath before I can say anything else equally stupid. "President Satchell is your father?" That can't be what she means. "You don't have the same last name."

"He's my stepdad. But he married my mom when I was a baby so he's the only dad I've ever known."

"Damn." I scratch the back of my neck, taking in that information. "Yeah, I guess that puts you under a lot of pressure then." And me, perhaps. President Satchell has been touted as the most conservative president this liberal school has had in years. I cringe at what Satchell would think if he knew his daughter had gotten it on with me in a storage room.

Kira shares the cringe. "Tell me about it. He's everywhere. And you think he has a conservative rep as a president? You should see him as a dad."

Everything suddenly falls into place. "You mean, he's the type of father who encourages his daughter to get involved with dad-approved on-campus groups. Like basket-weaving. Or Cherry Savers."

"There's no basket-weaving at UNC," she giggles. "Wait, maybe there is. Anyway, it wasn't *entirely* his decision that I join Cherry Savers. I did youth group with some of those girls in high school when my sister was acting out, and it seemed like a good idea to do this with them as a freshman. I'm just...not a freshman anymore."

Was *freshman* a euphemism? I shift in my seat. Talking about her virginity seems a little out of place considering this conversation is mostly about her dad. But I'm still curious. "What happened with your sister?"

Kira sits back in her chair. "She was a bit adventurous in high school. Slept with everyone. Now she's twenty-one with no degree, no husband, and two kids under three."

"Ah, I see." I frown. Bet her dad loves that. "That could definitely make celibacy seem attractive."

"It did. Now, not so much." She smiles shyly—and did she just scan her eyes down my torso?

Maybe it was wishful thinking. So I just raise a questioning brow.

"I realized that Mia's problem was with responsibility. I mean, all my friends were having sex and none of *them* were getting pregnant. Mia—that's my sister—"

"I figured."

"She really disappointed a lot of people." Kira's voice is suddenly heavy. "My parents, for example. I guess I overcompensated by being the good girl."

"Hmm." But... Now that I understand her reasons for keeping her virginity for so long, I find myself confused by why she'd decided to lose it.

"What's that supposed to mean?"

Of course that wasn't a question I really want to ask out loud. What if she tells me again that it had all been a mistake? "Nothing."

She nudges my leg with hers under the table, igniting that electricity again. "Come on. Tell me."

"Really, it's nothing." But that plea in her eyes...how could I not answer her? "Okay, okay, I was just wondering what made you decide to finally give it up."

"Then you believe me now? That I was a virgin?"

She nudges me again with her foot and I can't help nudging her back. "I told you I believed you back on the quad. Why would you lie?"

"Right?"

Now our feet are tangled together and I'm having a harder time focusing.

"So what's the answer?" I move my foot up and down her calf, noticing her eyes glint as I do so.

"I don't know." I scoot forward in my chair so that now it isn't just our lower legs touching, but our knees. I want to make hers weak. "I felt ready, I guess. Wanted to see what all the excitement was about. I was tired of feeling like I was left out of this secret club."

"I get that." I do not get that. I lost my virginity at fifteen, the first of my friends. There was no feeling left out for this guy. I was president of the secret club. But hey, I can empathize, right?

Besides, that wasn't really what I was asking her. And now that our legs are wrapped up together so intimately, I work up the courage to spell it out for her. "What I meant was, why did you decide to give it up *to me?*"

Kira meets my eyes with such an intense look that I feel dizzy. Jesus, that girl does a number on me. It's a really good feeling.

After a few seconds of that all-consuming gaze, she looks away and makes me suffer. "Ah, come on. A girl's got to have some secrets."

I miss her stare already. And the heat from where our legs were touching burns through my thighs to my groin. I want her. Again. There's no denying that.

But she deserves so much more—holding hands, footsies, dates at Open Mic Night. And if I have my way, I'll give it to her. All of it. But after the rocky start we've made, will she even want that from me? Or will I always be the guy who took her virginity, didn't take her number, and then guiltily bought her coffee six months later?

Kira wipes her mouth with a napkin and pushes her chair away from the table. "Are you ready?"

"Uh, sure. Where are we going?" *Please, God, don't let her send me home yet.* I'm not ready to leave her. I hold my breath while I wait for her response.

"You wanted to see the sights, right? I thought of someplace worth showing off."

Chase Matthews Is Having the Best Day of His Life.

FIVE

TEN MINUTES LATER, I'm strapping myself into the passenger seat of Kira's brand new Kia. Bet you can't say that five times fast. My dad's old Toyota Corolla is back at my house, while hers had just been up the block. Very convenient.

"Nice car," I tell her, as she pulls out of her parking space.

She glances at me before returning her eyes to the front windshield. "A present from Daddy when I made Princess Cherry Saver."

"It's even red, how fitting." I can't help but laugh at that. "So, do you have to give it back now?"

Kira scoffs. "I'm not telling him *anything*. Are you?"

"Hell, no. Authority figures scare the shit out of me as it is." No, I do not plan to tell the man anything at all. My head fills with images of things President Satchell could do to me.

Pull my scholarship. Throw me out of the Education Department. Or just plain kick me in the balls.

The last thought makes me glance around. School presidents don't employ spies, do they?

"Relax. He's not coming after you."

Damn, how does she read me like that? It's freaky and freaking cool all at the same time.

We stop at a red light and Kira gives me another once-over, this one quite obvious. "In fact, you're exactly the type of guy I could bring home and Dad *wouldn't* blow a gasket."

At first I can't decide if I should be grateful for the compliment or scared shitless. If any of my buddies had told me that their first date was talking about meeting her parents —I'd have told them to run far and fast. Funny now that I'm more curious than concerned.

Proud even.

I sit up taller in my seat, and return her up-down look. "What makes you think I'd be Daddy material?"

She laughs. "Oh, did you think that was a compliment?"

"You're kind of a bitch, you know that?" But I'm laughing with her. And it's real obvious from my tone that says I think she's anything but.

"Princess bitch, thank you very much." Now she's the proud one.

"I'm making you a T-shirt so everyone will know. It can replace the one you're wearing." I look down at the cherries on her chest that conveniently lie between her perfectly perky breasts. That awful slogan—*Life's Full of Pits, Save a Cherry*—taunts me. "I have to admit, that shirt on you drives me a little insane."

"Does it? I could take it off." Her sly grin suggests she has nothing but her bra on underneath.

And...there goes my cock. *Fanfuckingtastic.* Just when I'd gotten my last semi under control.

"No? I'll leave it on then." She pats my thigh. "But if you change your mind, let me know." And she winks.

My pants grow even tighter.

"Anyway..." I run a hand over my face and wonder how I should play this. Is she hoping for a repeat performance? Or is she simply being flirty? Or maybe she just likes seeing me in misery. Surely it's just a joke, regardless.

Now someone explain that to my dick.

I shift in my seat and try to think about something totally nonsexual. Like Jared. Or President Satchell.

Neither image helps. Truth is, they just aren't as potent in my mind as the intoxicating presence of Kira at my side. The totally hot, beautiful, amazing Kira Larson.

Shoot me now; I'm completely smitten. In the space of a single afternoon, how could I have gone from fantasizing about a stranger, to furious with a liar, to overwhelmed by my growing feelings for this complicated woman?

I shake my head and try to shove my emotions back into a box. She's given me no indication that this means anything more to her than a flirtatious afternoon. Won't help to mope about it, though. Regardless of what she's feeling, I get to be alone with her. What more could I want?

Well.

A bed would be nice.

Or at least someplace private. I glance out the window, noticing the total lack of well—anything. We seem to be in the middle of nowhere, on a rough road surrounded by fields and vacant plots of land. "So where are you taking me, anyway?"

Her devilish grin returns, accompanied by that twinkle in her eye that I'm starting to adore so much. "It's a surprise."

"Is this a good time to tell you I don't do well with surprises?" I do fine with surprises. I would simply prefer to not have been surprised by my growing affection for her. Or for what she could possibly be thinking about me.

"Too bad, because I'm not telling you." She glances at me just in time to see the disappointment flash across my face. Then, seeming to take pity, says, "It won't even make sense until you see it."

"Fine." I exaggerate a sigh. "But we barely know each other. Maybe I should send a text to my friends so they know to come looking for me in case you're headed to a kill room."

"Oh, I wouldn't say we don't know each other." And there's that wink again. "But you're right. I have the control here. I could kidnap you and no one would be the wiser."

"And what would you do to me then?" I was just going to play along, but I couldn't stop the sexual vibe in my voice if I wanted to. The thought of her tying me up and using me for her pleasure...

"Also a surprise."

I'm half disappointed that she isn't specific, half relieved for my erection.

But of course she goes on. "It would definitely be wicked and vile."

Still not specific, but it paints a certain sort of picture. "I like the sound of that." The picture grows more vivid in my mind—maybe she doesn't even wait for a secluded cabin.

Maybe she pulls over and rides me on the side of the road. "Maybe surprises aren't that bad after all."

And now I've gone past semi and straight for hard.

Conversation is definitely not working. Time for another distraction. I can hear the latest Twenty-One Pilots song beginning softly in the background and I grab onto it like a lifeline. "Can I turn this up? I love this song." My hand's already on the radio dial.

"I do, too!" Her eyes gleam. "Crank it."

We sing along to songs on the radio while Kira drives us further away from civilization. It helps me calm down, which I'm grateful for. After a few tunes, she turns at a crossroad with no markings. I have to wonder how in the hell she knows where she's going. Or *if* she knows where she's going. Not that I care if we have an actual destination, or if she just wants to get lost. The ride is totally worth it.

Soon, a large tree appears on the side of the road ahead. It's easy to spot from far away, being the only tall thing anywhere around us. As we get closer, I notice there's something odd about the tree—objects hanging from its bare branches. A few more feet nearer and it's plain that they aren't just any old objects, but shoes.

Shoes?

Kira slows the car and parks along the shoulder.

This is it? The only sight worth seeing in Greeley, Colorado?

She opens her door and turns to me. I haven't yet moved. "Well? Are you getting out?"

"Yeah. Yeah, I totally am." We can make out at the weird tree if that's what she's into. I unbuckle my seatbelt and venture out of the car.

Kira crosses to meet me in front of the hood. "It's cool, right?"

Cool isn't exactly the word that comes to mind. I tilt my head, squinting up against the afternoon sun, hoping to gain a better comprehension of what I'm looking at. Shoes dangle everywhere I look. Mostly old shoes, it seems. And almost all of them are shoes with laces, tied together and flung over the higher branches.

"Well?" Kira peers up at me expectantly.

Chase Matthews Is at a Loss for Words.

I cross my arms over my chest and lean back against the car. "I don't get it. Why do people do this?"

She shrugs. "No one really knows how it got started. Maybe someone was out here and decided to throw their old pair of sneakers up into the only tree for miles around. Who knows? But now people treat it like a wishing tree. The people who know about this place, that is. I mean, it's not a secret or anything. People just don't remember it's out here. But some people are pretty faithful about it. Every time my grandpa goes through a pair, he's out here wishing."

Somehow Kira's monologue clears up very little. "People throw their shoes up and make a wish? Like tossing a penny in a fountain?"

"Exactly like that." She nudges my shoulder with hers. "What are you thinking?"

"Honestly?" I don't want to offend her, but I'm not going to lie. Not about this. "I'm thinking this tradition is kind of weird."

Her eyes go wide in disbelief. "*Weird?* It's cool."

Shoes flung into a random tree in the middle of nowhere?

"It's weird. I always thought throwing your shoes on something like that meant there was a drug dealer nearby."

Kira puts a hand dramatically over her chest. "That is an urban legend! This? This is sweet and hopeful and even a little romantic."

"It's weird."

The car shifts as she sits on the hood. "Oh my God, you're totally going to ruin this place for me, aren't you?"

I move my eyes from the strange sight in front of me to Kira. Her shoulders are sagging and her expression is totally deflated. Shit. Not what I was going for. I'd thought we could laugh together, but I'd misread the situation—yet again. "No, no, no. I'm sorry. I'm not ruining anything. It's not weird." I put an arm around her and pull her into me.

She frowns, her lower lip thrust forward in a perfectly kissable pout. "You're pacifying me."

"Nope. I've gotten used to the idea now and it's not weird. I was wrong." It's totally still weird, but I'm not making the mistake of saying that again. Especially not now that she's leaning into me, and I can smell the soft scent of her shampoo.

As if she can read my mind, her pout turns into determination. "Prove it."

Um… I think fast and pull out my phone from my jacket pocket with one hand, click a picture of the shoe tree. "There. I'll even make that shot my lock screen." I'm not sure I know what she means by *prove it* but hopefully that does the trick.

"I don't mean like that. I mean, make a wish." Her expression is hopeful, her face lit up with pure delight. Like making a wish on the shoe tree was the most amazing thing a guy could do for her.

"Throw my shoes up there?" I'm considering it. I want to be that guy. Still…

I look down at my favorite broken-in pair of Converse. "I like these shoes. I need these shoes." My feet will be frozen by the time we get back. But I'll do it if I need to. After I mourn them for a few more minutes.

She giggles, and I can't help but steal a glance at the way her tits bounce with her laughter. "You don't need to throw your shoes. There are enough shoes up there to carry enough power for a few extra wishes. Just close your eyes and think about what you want. I'll even do it with you."

She closes her eyes and seems to concentrate. After a few seconds she opens one eye and peeks at me.

Whoops. I'm supposed to be wishing with her. I accidentally got too caught up in watching her while replaying her words in my mind. *Do it with you.* If she had any idea how badly I wanted her to do it with me again…

Kira slides out from under my arm as she turns her torso toward me, challenge written in her eyes. "You're thinking I'm being weird again, aren't you?"

"No. That's not what I was thinking." It was the furthest thing from my mind, actually. Besides having carnal thoughts about her, I'm also thinking about what a strange course my day has taken. From not being able to get the mystery girl out of my mind to seeing her at a purity rally to standing out in the middle of nowhere with her every action saying that she could want me as much as I want her.

Chase Matthews Is Thinking He's Pretty Damn Lucky.

"Then what *are* you thinking?" The breeze blows across the plain, her hair dancing across her face.

I shift toward her, tucking a lock of that sweetly scented

hair behind her ear. "I'm thinking I don't know what to wish for." I pause for a second, deciding whether it's too much too soon to say what I want to say. Deciding I don't care. "The thing I've been wishing for already came true."

"What was that?" Her voice is soft but expectant.

My eyes lock on hers so she can see that I mean this. "That I'd see you again."

Her breath catches—I actually hear it, the small little gasp she makes as I make my declaration. If that isn't a green light, then I must be color blind.

I turn my body so I'm facing her, where she's still sitting on the hood. Bracing my hands on the car on either side of her, I lean forward, my forehead nearly touching hers. "Now I have another wish."

"What?" It's barely a whisper, but it holds enough strength to make my balls twitch.

There's no going back now—I'm lost in her. Completely.

I move my hands from the car to her waist. "I wish I could show you what it's like to make love in a bed."

She tilts her chin up. "That's funny. That was my wish too."

"How about we make it come true?"

As my mouth meets hers, and I disappear into the motion of our lips and tongues gliding together, I have to admit that I really had been wrong: the shoe tree is anything but weird. It's all the things Kira had said it was—sweet and hopeful and a whole lot romantic.

SIX

ON THE DRIVE back to town, I can't stop touching Kira. I nuzzle and suck along her neck. My hands stroke her thighs through her jeans. At the few stoplights we hit when we get back into town, I claim her lips with deep, promising kisses. Except for the one horn honk we receive from a truck behind us when we linger too long in our embrace, she remains an excellent driver. It's surprising, considering how distracting I've been. But soon she won't be able to focus on anything but my touch.

In between kissing and fondling, I direct her to my place. She doesn't offer her home, and, since I assume she still lives with her parents, that's fine by me. I'd rather sneak around Jared and my other roommates than have to sneak around President Satchell.

Luckily, my bedroom is just off the kitchen, so we can slip through the back door and into my room without being seen. Also fortunate is the state I left my room in. It's semi-clean, except for the pile of dirty clothes, which I'm easily able to scoop up and throw into the closet.

Something about the walk from car to house, however, infuses a dose of awkward between us. We're no longer touching and I'm not exactly sure how to correct that.

I shut the door and click the lock into place. The sound echoes ominously through the quiet space. Maybe I shouldn't have locked the door. Was it too presumptuous?

"No, you're being prepared. It's all good."

Shit, I didn't mean to say that out loud. And why does Kira seem more comfortable than I do, already slipping out of her jacket? I'm supposed to be the expert here.

"Make yourself—" I start to say at the same time she says, "Nice place you—"

We laugh together and, damn, the anticipation of what else we could be doing together—*will* be doing together—has me stiff in the pants.

"You go first," I offer, not even remembering what it was I was going to say.

"Just...nice room." She peers up at me.

Maybe she's more nervous than I thought. Somehow, that makes me feel better.

"What were you going to say?"

I shake my head, the thought long gone by now. Besides, I don't want to say anything. I just want to kiss those incredibly pouty lips and wrap my hands around her perfectly round tits. I meet her eyes and hope that she can read all that in my gaze.

It must have worked.

Because the next thing I know, we're no longer standing several feet apart, but wrapped in each other. I'm not even sure who moved first, just that we've come together and that the feel of her in my arms is both natural and electrifying—how is that possible? Her lips burn me in such a fabulously amazing way, her tongue stirring the fire I feel singeing at my crotch. Her touch is searing and exquisite, like a hot shower. Like sitting by a blazing fire. Like drowning in heat.

I move quickly to take off her shirt—that ridiculous Cherry Saver T-shirt—then slow down, pulling away to gaze at her tits through the blue lace bra she still wears. Her breasts had stayed tucked away when we'd got it on in the storage room of the bar. Now I want to see them, to touch them. To properly experience them. I'm not going to be the "take my time" sort. My exploration of her body will take exactly what it will take, whether it be hurried or drawn out. But her breasts? Those require time to savor.

I start to reach behind to undo the clasp of her bra, but she stops me to do it herself. Which is hot. Watching her strip bare in front of me, displaying her beautiful chest with only a slight hint of shyness—totally hot. I reach out to touch them, grasping one in each hand.

Oh, God. The feel of them...tits never fail to get me going. Tits are amazing.

I flick my thumbs over Kira's nipples and she sighs. The sound snaps me out of my worship. I still have more worshiping to do—just maybe I can make it more comfortable for her.

I start to lead her over to my bed, but before I can lay her down, she tugs at my shirt. "Hey. Why am I the only one half naked?"

I pull my shirt off and toss it behind me. "The better question is: why are you only *half* naked?"

"I'll race you."

In a blur of clothes flying, both of us giggling, we scramble to remove the rest of our clothing. And there's the condom to put on. Then, our lips find each other again, and with our bodies pressed together we fall onto the bed.

"I think I won," Kira says, straddling me so that my dick knocks at her butt cheeks.

It's hard to concentrate with my throbbing erection so close to the goal, but I clear my head enough for a short conversation. "It wasn't a fair race. You weren't wearing socks."

I run my hands up and down her upper legs, totally trans-fixed by her shapely thighs and the vee in the middle where they meet her torso. My thumb reaches up to rub the bump hidden in between her folds.

Her back arches at my touch. "How about I share the prize, then?" Her voice is breathy and uneven.

"Fantastic idea." After sliding my fingers low enough to discover the moisture pooled at her hole, I flip her under-neath me and position myself at her entrance. "I hope your idea of the prize is the same as mine."

"Can you stop talking about it and stick it in already?"

Too horny to laugh, I make a mental note to dwell on my appreciation of her candor at another time and abide by her instruction. I slide in—carefully, more cautiously than the last time. Closing my eyes, I still, enjoying the feel of her tight walls encased around my dick.

Kira has other ideas, bucks her hips beneath me. "Move!"

"I'm moving. I'm moving." And I am. Gliding in and out of her with rhythmic thrusts. Vaguely I remember that I'd thought being inside Kira Larson was like being in heaven. I was wrong. There's no way heaven could be this good, this perfect, this fanfuckingamazing. And maybe that's blasphemous to think, but it's the goddamn truth.

From the look of it, Kira agrees. She writhes and wriggles, digging her fingernails into my shoulders all the while making those sexy little moans that have been permanently seared into my memory. The bed jostles with our movement, but thankfully doesn't squeak. Squeaking beds are definitely hot, but the sound would carry and attract nosy roommates. Plus, I might miss the hotter sound of slapping thighs as I pick up the speed of my thrusts.

"Can you feel me getting harder for you?"

"Yeah. Yeah, I can." Kira wraps her legs around me and locks her mouth to mine.

The new position is going to do me in. "God, Kira, I'm going to come."

"Me, too. Me, too." She squeezes around me just as my climax surges through me.

I groan out her name. This time I don't think it's weird, but right. Yeah, it's exactly right.

Kira Larson Is Exactly Right.

WE DOZE FOR A LITTLE, tangled in each other's arms. When I wake, Kira is watching me, her eyes and smile saying she's content. At least, that's what I think they're saying.

"Hi." She runs her hand through my hair.

It feels so perfect to have her there beside me. I dread the thought of the day ending. A quick glance at the clock on the nightstand says it's almost nine in the evening.

Without even giving it a second thought, I draw her closer and ask the question I'm dying to ask. "Can you stay here tonight? Or will Satchell send out campus police if you miss curfew?"

"I don't live with my parents, asshole." She nips playfully at my ear. "I live with my sister."

"With Mia?" I hope I'm impressing her with my memory.

"You remembered her name." She rewards me with a peck at the side of my mouth. "Yeah, since the beginning of the summer. I help her take care of her kids during the week when I'm not in class."

I feel like a cad for not knowing that. We still have so much to learn about each other. But if she stays, we can keep learning all through the night. "And the weekends?"

"Are mine, free and clear." She stretches her hands above her head, the movement showing off her awesome tits. "And no, she doesn't check up on me. So, yes. I'll stay." She wraps her arms around my neck, cuddling into me.

I turn my torso to press against her. "You don't know how happy that makes me."

"I could find out." Kira's hand is already traveling downward.

I stop her by grabbing her wrist. I mean, I *am* hard again and eager for another round, except our activities have worked up quite an appetite. "Yes, you could. And I would be glad to show you, but first..." As if on cue, my stomach growls. "Are you hungry?"

She giggles. "Starving. But I don't want to go anywhere."

She's so adorable. Her comfort level around me, the sound of her laughter, her pouty lips—I regret my need for food.

But she's staying the night! So a timeout for dinner is tolerable.

I swing my legs off the bed, find my jeans, and quickly pull them on, skipping the underwear. "I'll go raid the kitchen."

Kira points to where she'd flung her clothing. "Hand me my T-shirt. I'll come help you."

"No, no, no. Not a good idea. The guys might be home." I can just imagine the harassment we'd suffer. I don't mind so much for myself, but Kira doesn't deserve to meet them like this. Especially since I intend to have her around in the future. A lot, if I have my way about it.

I glance down at the girl in my bed and realize her smile has disappeared. Shit! I hadn't meant that the way she apparently assumed.

I lean down, putting a hand on her shoulder, and kiss her temple. "I know what you're thinking and it's wrong. I'm not embarrassed by you. I'm not ashamed to have you here. I'd like to shout to the whole world that Kira Larson is naked in my bedroom." I pause for her to smile. "But my roommates are assholes and I don't want to force you through an encounter with them. If you want to still join me, it's up to you."

She bites her lip as she considers. "How about I stay here and keep the bed warm?"

"That sounds like a fabulous idea."

I manage to make it in and out of the kitchen without anyone seeing me. I can hear some of the guys in the other room shooting pool. They sound like they're having a good time. But I'll bet they aren't having near as good of a time as I'm having.

I return to my room with an armful of snack foods and two cans of pop. "Sorry. We're guys. There's not much to choose from."

Kira sits up against the headboard. "You've got Doritos, and that's all I need."

"A girl after my own heart." I sit on the bed facing her and spread the snacks between us. I grab a handful of chips and pass the bag to her.

While I was gone, she'd gotten her shirt off the floor and was now wearing it. That silly, ridiculous slogan teases me. "So." I nod toward her shirt. "Are you still going to be a Cherry Saver?"

Kira waits to swallow before answering. "I'll finish up my reign this year, yeah." About to pop another chip in her mouth, she pauses. "Will that bother you?"

I think about it. "Except that you aren't completely naked at the moment, nothing about you bothers me."

Her eyes twinkle. "You're not naked either."

This is true. I stand and remove my jeans. Putting my hands out in a ta-da pose, I declare, "Now I am."

Kira pulls off her T-shirt, throws it aside, and mimics my pose. "So am I."

"Awesome." *So awesome.* It's so cool how she isn't shy around me. Lots of girls like to cover up and play prude, even after we've done the horizontal hustle. Kira seems comfortable with her body and I like that.

I think for a moment about her question from earlier. "As for the Cherry Saver thing, it really *doesn't* bother me." It is odd, though. Will I have to pretend that we're just friends when I see her in public? Can she even hang around me in public? Does she even want to?

I take a swallow of my pop and try to figure out the best way to address all my questions. "I just need to know how to play it."

She shrugs. "Discreetly, I guess."

Well, that isn't saying much. I'll have to be more forward. "Like, can you date? Are you allowed to hold hands? Can you kiss in front of other people?" Mustering my courage, I add, "Can *I* kiss you in front of other people?"

"Of course. I'm not a monk." She pours a handful of peanuts into her hand from the jar I had brought in. She seems to consider for a minute. "Truth?"

I nod.

"Half the Cherry Savers are sexually active."

Huh. I guess Jared *was* right about the rep of the girls in the group. He's still a douche, though.

"But as Princess, I should try harder to maintain appearances." Her cheeks pink up and she peers at me from under lowered lids. "But I'm definitely hoping you'll kiss me in front of other people."

"Then, I will." I grin, feeling more elated than I probably should. "I'll kiss you whenever you let me."

Still, the whole thing is a little phony. "If you're all putting out, why do you even join? Isn't that a bit..." I trail off, not sure what word to use that won't offend her.

"Hypocritical?"

Thank God she'd said it for me. "Yeah, that."

"Maybe. But there are lots of good values we focus on besides purity."

"Such as...?"

"Like, how to handle pressure to put out. Not using sex as a way to judge your worth. Waiting for the right person." Her eyes gleam as she talks. "Admittedly, some people are only there to please their parents or have an organization on their resume. But others take it seriously to varying degrees."

I think I'm starting to understand. "You mean, some of you are just okay with oral, and some go all the way?"

"Yeah, like that."

"And your experience with oral...?" I have to ask. It's in the Dude Handbook, I'm pretty certain.

"Look at you, Mr. Reporter. Are you conducting an interview for one of your articles?"

I feel a passing stab of guilt in my chest. I'm obviously not doing the journalism piece on her anymore, but I *had* come pretty darn close. Thank God I'd come to my senses. Otherwise I'd be forever looking in the past with Kira and not toward the future as I am now.

Of course, she doesn't know about the story I'd planned. She's just teasing me. "Yeah, that's right. An exclusive tell-all interview with a princess and daughter of the president." I wait for her to laugh. "No, I'm just curious. I lost my virginity kind of early."

Her eyes narrow.

"I wasn't a slut," I amend. "But I've always been active, so Cherry Savers is totally out of my realm of understanding. And I'm truly interested in whether or not you give blowjobs. Because I'm totally a guy, if you haven't noticed."

"Oh, I noticed." It's sexy the way her brows waggle and her voice drips with sultry tones. "And you'll just have to wait and find out whether I'm educated in the ways of BJs. But chances are you won't have to wait terribly long."

I can't stop grinning. Not just because she's suggesting she'll go down on me in the future, but because of everything she says and is. She's cute and spunky and beautiful and super sexy. She's a hundred things I always liked in girls and another hundred things I never knew I liked. As I gaze at her, adoration likely written all over my face, I can't help but wonder how I got so fortunate as to end up with her. How she'd ended up picking *me*, of all the guys she could have, to be with intimately.

She blushes under my stare. "What?"

"Why me?"

"Why you, what?"

I push our picnic aside so I can stretch out next to her. "Why did you save yourself for me?" She hadn't known me so maybe that's not the right phrasing. "Or would you have hooked up with any guy that walked into that bar that night?"

She opens her mouth to say something, then shuts it again.

"It's okay if that's the answer." I sure *hope* that isn't the answer. "I just want to know."

Kira looks down at her hands. "I went there to find a guy."

"Oh." I know my disappointment shows in my voice.

"But..." She scoots down so we're both horizontal, facing each other. "I'd been going there all summer looking for a guy."

She'd been going there all summer. "Really?" I'm surprised. And delighted.

Or maybe I'm taking it wrong. Maybe I was her only choice. "No other offers?"

Kira pushes my chest. "I had plenty of other offers, thank you very much."

Dammit, I always say the wrong thing. "I'm sorry! I

totally didn't mean it like that. Of course you had other offers. I'm betting men were lining up for you." How could they not? She's perfect.

I reach out to brush a strand of hair off her face. "I didn't mean to sound surprised about that. It's me I'm surprised about. Why was *I* the guy?"

"Stop ragging on yourself. You're pretty hot. You know that, right?" She pins me with her velvet browns.

"No." I know I'm all right looking, but *hot*? I can't say that I've ever been called that. I like it, that's for sure. Especially coming from her.

"Well, you are." There's that blush again. "But that wasn't why."

"Then why?"

She shakes her head. "It's silly."

"Tell me." When she still protests, I decide to play dirty, grabbing her wrists with one hand and tickling her.

"Stop! Stop!" She's breathless when I let up. "Okay, fine." She takes a deep breath, still recovering from my attack. "Remember when you were trying to teach me how to play pool? And you put your arms around me?"

I do remember that. I'd reached around to help her get the right action with her cue. It had been the first time I'd touched her that night and it was magic. "There were sparks. Right? Because I totally felt sparks."

"There were sparks." Her face sparkles with the memory. "But that wasn't it."

God, then what the hell was it?

"It was what you said when I missed the shot. Do you remember?"

"I'm not sure." I remember a lot of things I said that night

—like, "Wanna find some place more private?" and "God, Kira, you feel good." But nothing comes to mind that was out of the ordinary or especially interesting.

"You said, 'That's okay. On our next date, we'll play again and you'll play better.'" She raises her eyes to meet mine. "You talked about the future and not just hooking up for the night. You made me feel like you would have waited for me. That's how I knew you were the one."

Warmth spreads through my body despite the fact that I'd just been feeling a bit chilly what with no clothes on and all. I had talked to her about the future because, even early in the evening, I'd really hoped to see her again. She'd been cool and fun and different from a lot of the girls I knew in San Diego.

And all this time I thought I'd been the only one feeling it, she'd felt the same way. "Then why didn't you give me your phone number after?"

She takes my hand, laces her fingers through mine and squeezed. "Why didn't you ask?"

"Because I was a chickenshit. I was afraid you'd turn me down." I let go of her hand so I can pull her close to me. "And I didn't want to ruin the night with a bad ending."

"Hmm." She closes her eyes, as if taking my words in. After a moment she says, "I like that."

"I like you." My body presses flush against hers, so she has to already know. The evidence is jabbing her in the thigh.

But I have more that she doesn't know. More that I want her to hear before I slide inside her for the second time tonight. "And I would have waited for you. I'm so glad you waited for me."

I don't give her much opportunity to respond with words

as I roll her underneath me and tell her all the things my body can say much better than my mouth.

And, with her moans and sighs and the way her body reacts to my attention, I can feel her saying, "I'm glad I waited for you, too."

SEVEN

KIRA and I stayed up late into the night, talking and...other things. So it isn't surprising that we sleep in the next morning. Activity in the kitchen wakes me up. I look over at the sleeping beauty next to me and consider curling back up in her warmth. But the need to pee gets me out of bed and heading to my private bathroom.

As I'm leaving the john, I hear the knob rattle on the bedroom door. Thank God I had locked it. Jared has no boundaries. And if I don't address him now, he'll never leave.

I grab a towel off the bathroom rack and wrap it around my waist. Then I open the door, but only enough for conversation.

As I guessed, it's Jared standing on the other side.

"What's up?" I try to be quiet without seeming like I'm being quiet. Like I'd told Kira, I'm not embarrassed to be seen with her, but I want to respect her privacy.

Jared tries to peer over my shoulder, obviously curious

about why he isn't being let in the room. "Hey, I didn't hear you come in last night."

"I wasn't feeling very social so I snuck in the back and went to bed early." Well, it's somewhat true. I *had* felt social, just on a one-on-one basis. And the part about going to bed early *was* dead on.

"Huh. Okay." Jared again tries to peek in. But the bed isn't visible from his vantage point so he seems to zero in on what he can see instead. He nods at my towel. "Are you getting in the shower or do you sleep naked?"

I want to say, *"None of your fucking beeswax,"* but instead settle for something more roommate-friendly. "Why? Are you trying to check out my dick?"

"Shut up. I only wondered if there was a special reason for the attire. Nudge, nudge, wink, wink."

Jesus, isn't it supposed to be girls who have the nosey reputation? I am not filling in Jared on my night with Kira. Especially when she's still sleeping behind me. Thinking of her still in bed, I long to join her. "Did you need something, Jared?"

Jared leans against the doorframe. Dammit, he's making himself comfortable. "Not really. Just checking in on you."

"And I'm fine. So, maybe we can talk later. Like, when I'm dressed." I know I sound snippy, but come on. We're friends, but I still deserve some privacy.

"Sure. Later, then." Except Jared makes no move to leave. "Hey, are you avoiding me?"

"No!" Just what I need—Jared to go all butt hurt.

"Then why are you being all weird and shit?"

I sigh. Better to smooth things over. "I'm being weird? I

didn't realize. I haven't had any coffee yet or a shower so I'm still half asleep."

"Yeah. Yeah. Okay. Got it. I'll let you wake up." Jared turns to go, then suddenly flips back to me. "Oh! How did you make out with that Princess Cherry Saver?"

I stiffen, and not where I want to be stiffening. Did Jared know I'd hooked up with Kira again? I don't want her to think I'd only approached her with the intention of making it back to this room.

I lower my voice. "Uh, what do you mean?"

Jared does not follow suit, and continues at full volume. "You know. The story."

I really must not be quite awake. Or I'm still lost in the fog of Kira because there's some warning bell going off in the back of my head but I can't seem to register what it is.

And without me stopping him, Jared keeps on talking. "That article you were gonna write about her not being a virgin? The exposé?"

Oh, yeah. *That.*

And I don't have to wonder long if Kira is hearing this conversation.

"Exposé?" She stands behind me, wrapped in my comforter.

I turn and meet her eyes. In the span of a few seconds, her expression morphs through confusion, understanding, and finally settles on hurt.

God, seeing pain in Kira's eyes was never what I'd intended.

And now her expression is changing again—to rage.

Panic runs through me like a wildfire. "No, Kira, it's not what it sounds like. I mean, I was going to write about you and Cherry Savers and not having your cherry, but that was—"

"You were planning to tell *everyone* about what happened at the bar?" Her tone is drowning in fury.

I can't deny it. Jared is right behind me, and had already spilled the truth. No, I'll just have to be honest and hope for the best. "Yes, but not after—"

Honesty seems to not have been the most successful course of action. Kira is already gathering her clothes off the floor.

"Stop. Talk to me." My pleading doesn't halt her in the least. I step in front of her, one hand on her shoulder, the other still gripping the towel at my waist. "Come on, Kira. I can explain."

She meets my eyes and I almost wish she hadn't. It isn't just rage I can see there, but pain. "Were you or were you not going to expose a very private thing about me—a thing that would hurt and embarrass me—to the entire school? *Slut-shaming* me in a way that could follow me for the rest of my life?"

With all my heart I want to say I wouldn't have done it. But at one point, for at least an hour of my day, I had planned on it. Sincerely planned on doing this awful thing, that's so much more awful when I look at it through her eyes. I lower mine. "Yes. I was."

Kira brushes past me into the bathroom.

I follow after her. "But I changed my mind." She slams the door in my face, nearly hitting me in the nose.

Jared chuckles behind me, reminding me that we have an audience. I turn and glare at my roommate, but that's all the energy I have to expend on Jared for the moment. My concern is Kira.

Speaking at the door between us, I continue to beg for forgiveness. "I'm sorry, Kira. It was a stupid lack of judgment on my part. But I didn't do it. I wouldn't have done it." God, I hope she believes me when I'm not so sure that's the whole truth. If we hadn't gone out to coffee, if she hadn't been so charming and fun, would I have still abandoned my quest?

I can't be sure.

The door opens and for a moment my spirits rise.

But Kira isn't coming out to talk to me. She's dressed and ready to leave.

Chase Matthews Fucked This All Up.

"Kira, wait." While she looks for her keys and boots, I scramble to find a pair of jeans. "Let me explain. Or make it up to you. I'm sorry!"

Without so much as a goodbye, she brushes past Jared and is out the door.

Fuck! I don't even bother to do up my pants as I follow after her. "Goddammit, Jared," I say as I shove roughly past him.

"Hey. I didn't know anyone was here. Maybe you should have told me." Jared obviously finds the whole thing entertaining. I'm going to look for a new place to live as soon as I straighten this mess out.

"Jesus." I curse under my breath, running out the back door after the girl I've become pretty attached to. "Kira, wait!"

But she's already peeling out of the driveway.

"Damn, that girl drives fast." Jared had apparently followed me outside. "In more ways than one." He laughs.

"Shut up, Jared."

"Sorry, man."

Even though Jared's apology doesn't sound all that sincere, if I'm being honest, it's myself I'm actually mad at. After all, everything he had said in that doorway was true.

I sit down on the chilly back step, and shake my head. "It's not your fault. I should have come clean earlier. I shouldn't have even planned it in the first place." It would have been a really shitty thing to do. I see that now. Even if I hadn't expected to get with Kira again, how could I do that to anyone, let alone a girl I'd gotten it on with?

Yeah, I've fucked up. Fucked up bad. "Now what do I do?" I ask, more to myself than Jared.

But Jared has an answer regardless. "Um, say farewell and bang one of the fifty other hotties that hit on you this week. I can still get you Wanna Blow's number."

I shoot Jared a glare that I hope reads, *die now*.

Instead, it must have read, *lovesick*, because Jared says, "Shit, you like this one."

I run my hand through my hair. "Yeah. I really do." God, I'm pathetic. I've only known the chick for about a day and I'm already this into her—major pathetic. I don't even know how to find her again. But yet again, I failed to procure her phone number. Except for knowing that it wasn't at home, I have no idea where she lives. I don't know the classes she was taking and, at the rally, the next Cherry Savers meeting had been announced for a whole month in the future.

And even if I do find her, how can I ever fix this?

With no one else around, I look up at Jared, as if *he'd* have a solution to my problem.

"Hey, I can't help you on this one. I'm a player, dude. I

don't do any of that romance stuff." Jared sits on the step next to me. "But my grandma used to always say that whatever the thing was that got you into the trouble in the first place is also the thing that is often the solution."

I start to ask what the fuck that's supposed to mean when it hits me like a ton of bricks—an idea to reach out to Kira and apologize at the same time. "Jared, that's brilliant."

"It is?" Jared probably isn't called brilliant too often. He seems to adjust to the title fast. "Of course it is. I'm great with advice."

"I'll be in my room the rest of the day," I tell him, eager to start on my plan. "I have an article to write."

EIGHT

I HADN'T BEEN sure the editor of the UNC paper would accept my article. After all, I hadn't written about campus life as requested, but I believe the piece I've come up with will be of interest to the student body.

The editor reads it in front of me, without so much as an eyebrow lift to indicate his approval or disapproval. When he finishes, the editor sets his copy on his desk and says, "It will run in the next issue which comes out Thursday. We rotate our editorial writers, so your next piece will be due two weeks from now."

I breathe a sigh of relief. Getting a job on the paper *had* been my original goal for writing the article, but now it's my chance to get Kira's attention. If the editor had decided not to print it, it would be back to the drawing board.

With the first part of my plan in place, now I just have to sit back and wait.

SURE AS THE editor had said, my piece appears in the next issue. But Thursday comes and goes with no word from Kira. Friday brings no word from her either. By Saturday, I'm beginning to lose hope. I thought for sure I'd have heard from her by now, if I was going to at all. So maybe this is it. She doesn't forgive me. And I've lost my chance forever.

Claiming too much homework, I stay behind when the rest of the guys go out to play Frisbee golf on Saturday afternoon. Truth is, I know that if by some miracle Kira *is* going to reach out to me, it would be at the house, and I don't want to miss her. How pathetic am I to keep wishing?

Pretty damn pathetic. But it doesn't change anything.

Deciding fresh air would be beneficial to my mood, I sit on the front porch trying to work on a paper for my Disabilities in Learning class. But my mind is too wrapped up in Kira to get anything done. Maybe she hasn't seen my piece. Maybe she had seen it and it hadn't made a difference. Maybe she hadn't been as interested in me as I'd thought in the first place. But that couldn't be the case—I'd *felt* the connection between us.

Hadn't I?

Each time a car pulls into the busy gravel lot next door, my ears perk up. Each time I'm rewarded with disappointment. Kira isn't coming. Better give up the dream and face the reality.

But then, after nearly an hour of unproductivity as the air grows chillier around me, the sound of a familiar engine pulls me from my moping. The guys had walked to their destination. Can it be...her? I listen to a single door slam shut and hold my breath while I wait for the driver to appear.

And then there she is—standing at the end of the front walk, a copy of the newspaper clutched in her hand.

Fuck, have I fallen asleep? Because she looks just like a dream.

But, no. She isn't a dream. She's real. And that's better than any dream I could imagine.

I don't know what to say, and my breath hasn't really returned anyway so speaking is pretty much out of the question. Besides, I'd had the last word when I wrote that article. It's Kira's turn to speak.

She's quiet, though, as she walks up to where I sit on the steps. She turns the paper to face me, the picture I'd snapped on my phone at the wishing tree prominent on the page. "You wrote this?" she asks.

Well, obviously. It says *by Chase Matthews* right under the headline: *Greeley's Shoe Tree.*

I nod.

Kira turns the paper back to face her and begins reading out loud. *"In a hard-to-find location on the back roads of Greeley exists one of the town's little known highlights—a shoe tree where sneakers are recycled for wishes."*

Skipping past a few paragraphs, Kira continues, *"While at first, the idea of wishing on shoes seemed odd to this reporter, further reflection thinks the tradition is actually apropos. The wishes we hold in our heart come out of our day-to-day routines. What other objects are more closely tied to our daily lives than the shoes that we walk in? They carry us wherever we go. Why shouldn't they be the items that we'd expect to carry us to our dreams, as well?"*

Kira pauses, glancing over at me.

Does she think she doesn't have my attention? She does. She always has.

She skips to the end of the piece. *"Even if you don't have a pair of shoes to dispose of, I believe the tree has power simply by being in its presence. The wish I made standing at the shoe tree came true in the most beautifully fulfilling way. Most writers would take this time to caution the readers about being careful about what they wish for. My caution, however, is different: be careful what we do with our wishes when they do come true. The shoes on the tree may carry us to the place we dream of, but our own feet can carry us back away. From personal experience, I can attest that any wish can be canceled as easily as it is made, usually because our ego gets in the way. I'm hoping that even canceled wishes can be made again."*

It was as close to an apology as I could have written in an article meant for the entire student body. Of course, it had really only been meant for Kira.

She folds the paper and sets it on the step beside her. Still not looking at me directly, she says, "I should be mad that you've disclosed my favorite secret spot."

Shit! I hadn't thought of that. But I hadn't written exactly how to get there—I don't exactly know myself. "God, Kira, I'm sorry—"

She cuts me off, "But I'm not." She swallows. "It was a good article. Thank you for writing it."

It doesn't seem like a fitting time to say, *"You're welcome,"* when there are other things I need to say. "Kira, I was an ass. Completely out of line. I shouldn't have ever considered outing you, and I understand how that could make me someone that wouldn't ever deserve your time and attention."

She shakes her head. "Whatever. Like I'm all that special."

"You *are* a princess."

She smiles. It's encouraging that I can still joke with her.

"You *are* that special," I continue. "And I regret that I even considered exploiting that."

"I may have overreacted." She puts her hand on the step between us.

Hoping that's a message, I place my hand over hers. "No. You gave me what I deserved." She doesn't pull away—in fact, she turns her palm up to clasp mine properly.

She pivots to meet my eyes—God, those beautiful brown eyes are entrancing. Especially when they are empty of the anger and hurt that had filled them the last time I saw them. I'm not sure what emotion I see in them this time, but whatever it is, it makes me feel warm all over.

"I think you deserve a whole lot more."

I try to hide my disappointment. I suffered greatly this whole week wondering if I'd ever get a chance to be with Kira again. I'd go through more, if I had to. She's worth it. "Any punishment you think I should have, bring it on. I'll endure it. Just don't say I can't see you again."

She laughs. "You don't want to know what kind of punishments I can come up with. Let's see..." She taps her lip with her finger as she appears to think of cruel and unusual methods of torture.

For some reason, I'm not worried.

After a second, Kira shakes her head. "Actually, that's not what I meant. I meant, you deserve a lot more good things."

I can think of a few good things that I'd like to have, but that I'm not necessarily worthy of. "I don't deserve you.

But that won't stop me from wishing for you over and over."

"Stop wishing. I'm here." She squeezes my hand.

How can such a simple gesture be felt all the way down in my balls? The electricity between us is high voltage.

She turns her body toward me so our knees are touching. Maybe she's as eager for more contact as I am. "I saved myself for you, remember? I'm yours for the taking."

Mine for the taking? I like the sound of that. From the twitch in my pants, my dick has ideas exactly where I could be taking her. And more specifically, when I should be taking her there.

With all the physical response going on with my body, I haven't said anything out loud. My silence seems to concern Kira. She lowers her eyes and says, "If you want me, that is."

"Yeah, I want you." Right now I want her pretty damn badly. But this conversation is about building a relationship based on more than sex. At least, I hope it is. Not for the first time since I met Kira, I wonder what's happened to me.

Well, might as well go all in. "I told the whole campus that I believe in a wishing tree. Would I have done that if I wasn't totally into you?"

Kira nods to the paper between us. "Are you saying you don't really believe this?"

"Oh, no. I believe. I'll never be able to find that place again even if my life depended on it, so I spent all week wishing on this dang photo of that tree instead." I lean my head in closer to hers. "And it worked. Because here you are."

I let my lips brush hers softly before moving in for a deeper kiss. I don't want her to think I'm only interested in her physically. It's a kiss that shows affection, not lust. My tongue remains shallow as it slips into her mouth. My hands stay wrapped around her waist, even though they long to wander. It takes great restraint not to take it further, but I somehow stay strong.

When I pull away, her eyes are big and her lips pink. Pink kisses...that reminds me of something. I run my thumb across her cheek in a sweet caress. "It's Valentine's Day. Will you be mine?"

Kira twists her lip in that ultra-sexy way of hers—man, she's killing me. "If I say yes, does that mean I'm going to get laid?"

Chase Matthews Is in Love.

ALL YOU NEED IS
LOVE

ALSO BY LAURELIN PAIGE

DON'T KNOW WHAT TO READ NEXT? LET ME HELP.

(Visit my website for a complete list and more detailed reading order.)

Want an edgy billionaire romance that pushes limits? Meet Donovan in **Dirty Duet:** Dirty Filthy Rich Men | Dirty Filthy Rich Love

How about a restless playboy who ends up falling for the last woman he should fall for: his fiancé. Then read the **Dirty Games Duet:** Dirty Sexy Player| Dirty Sexy Games

In the mood for a rich Brit and a much younger artist? Grab the **Dirty Sweet Duet:** Sweet Liar | Sweet Fate

If you like billionaire romance like Sylvia Day's Crossfire Series read **Fixed Series:** Fixed on You | Found in You | Forever with You | Hudson | Fixed Forever

If you like sexy lover's angst **Found Duet:** Free Me | Find Me

If you like dark romantic suspense, read ***First and Last*** First Touch | Last Kiss

If power dynamics, head games and kinky, edgy angst is your thing, read **Slay Series:** *Slay One: Rivalry | Slay Two: Ruin | Slay Three: Revenge | Slay Four: Rising*

Not ready to commit to a series? I have several **STANDALONES** *that can be read in any order:*

Chandler - *a light, billionaire romance*

Falling Under You - *a 35k novella featuring a strong woman and an alpha-beta male*

Dirty Filthy Fix - *a kinky little story that crosses over from the Dirty Universe to the Fixed Universe*

The Open Door - *another kinky exploration, this time of a happily married couple*

One More Time - *a second chance romance between two movie stars*

Close - *a hot young rock star falls for an older Hollywood A-lister*

Sex Symbol - *a contemporary romance that takes place on a movie set*

Star Struck - *another contemporary romance that takes place in Hollywood*

Happy Valentine's Day

ABOUT LAURELIN PAIGE

With millions of books sold, Laurelin Paige is the NY Times, Wall Street Journal, and USA Today Bestselling Author of the Fixed Trilogy. She's a sucker for a good romance and gets giddy anytime there's kissing, much to the embarrassment of her three daughters. Her husband doesn't seem to complain, however. When she isn't reading or writing sexy stories, she's probably singing, watching shows like Game of Thrones, Letterkenny and Discovery of Witches, or dreaming of Michael Fassbender. She's also a proud member of Mensa International though she doesn't do anything with the organization except use it as material for her bio.

www.laurelinpaige.com
laurelinpaigeauthor@gmail.com

Made in the USA
Columbia, SC
10 April 2021